BLACK TIDE

Note: *The Caledonian Canal connects the lochs that lie between Inverness and Fort William.*

BLACK TIDE

CAROLINE CLOUGH

 Kelpies

With love to my wonderful husband,
and my children, Charlotte and Rory.

Many thanks to my girls Julie and Sheila, who have supported
me so well for so long.

Thanks to all at Floris for their advice and support.

And thanks to all the lovely and enthusiastic pupils and
teachers that I have met in schools all over the country, who have
encouraged and inspired me to write Toby's new adventures in this
sequel to Red Fever.

 This book is also available
as an eBook

JF

Kelpies is an imprint of Floris Books

First published in 2012 by Floris Books
© 2012 Caroline Clough

Caroline Clough has asserted her right under the
Copyright, Designs and Patent Act 1988 to be
identified as the Author of this Work

The publisher acknowledges subsidy
from Creative Scotland towards the
publication of this volume

British Library CIP data available
ISBN 978-086315-877-3

Printed in Great Britain
by CPI Group (UK) Ltd, Croydon

1. Kidnapped

Something was wrong. In the fuggy state between slumber and waking, Toby Tennant could sense something was very wrong with his world. He tried to open his eyes but sleep had a strong grip on him and he couldn't shake it loose.

Wake up! I must wake up!

With a huge effort he squinted out of one eye, rubbing the other with a grimy hand. Blackness was all around him and for a moment he couldn't work out where he was. He groped for the torch that was tucked in beside him and, grasping the handle, quickly wound it up. It threw a pale flickering light on the inside of the tiny cabin.

Ah, I'm in my den.

For a moment he was reassured. This was his safe place, the place where he could hide from the madness outside that was now his life. But as he lay curled up on the old mattress that took up most of the space, he felt a growing unease. There was something *so* wrong with the way the boat was pitching and rolling sideways. Toby hated sailing, but the deadly red fever virus had changed everything over the past three years. He'd had to learn the ways of the sea in order to survive.

A terrible sense of dread crept over him and, fighting his terror, he pulled on his damp clothes. There was no sound from the *Lucky Lady*'s engine; there was no sound of his Dad or his little sister, Sylvie. There was no sound of anything or anybody, just the whack, whack, whack of the waves hitting the side of the boat as it was tossed and thrown about.

What's going on? Why aren't we moving? The boat feels like it's drifting. What's Dad doing?

Toby crawled to the hatch door and flipped it open, shading his eyes to the brightness of the morning light. As he swung round to face the *Lucky Lady*'s cabin he saw exactly what was wrong. There, stood on the deck, were two huge men dressed in black, their backs towards him. Toby froze, the cold hand of fear closing over his heart.

"Hey! You two! Come in here and help me tie the prisoners up!" shouted a gruff voice from inside the cabin.

"Yep, Captain!" The huge men stooped and disappeared through the low wooden door of the boat's cabin.

Prisoners? He must be talking about Dad and Sylvie. We've been boarded by pirates!

Toby now saw the grey outline of a large inflatable boat moored alongside the *Lucky Lady*. He pulled himself up onto the deck and, grasping the rail, made his way unsteadily towards the cabin as the boat bucked and shifted under his feet.

What are they doing with Dad and Sylvie? What do they want with them? Surely they just want to steal our food and fuel? Or maybe they aren't ordinary pirates.

A hot anger rose in Toby's chest as he imagined the dirty rough men pulling Sylvie around. She was only six years old and, though she could be very annoying at times, Toby was always fiercely protective of her. After all, she had no mum to look after her now.

What am I going to do? There are at least three of them and they are enormous and probably have weapons! How am I going to fight them off?

He slunk down and crawled nearer to the cabin door. He could hear raised voices from within.

"Take your filthy hands off us!" An angry voice rang out. It was his dad. "Why are you doing this? What do you want with us? Just take our food and fuel!"

Toby heard a loud, coarse laugh and then someone said, "We don't want your meagre offerings! It's YOU we want!"

There was a scream from Sylvie, and sounds of a scuffle came from the open door. Toby's blood started to boil. How dare these evil men board their boat and assault his family? He had to do something and he had to do it now. He glanced round searching for a weapon and spied a large wooden pole with a hook on the end, for pulling the boat up to moorings. He picked it up and, without thinking, flung himself through the cabin door.

What he saw inside made him cry out in fear and dismay. His dad and Sylvie were cowering in terror on one of the bunk beds, their hands tied in front of them. Standing over them were four men, filling the tiny cabin with their bulky frames. All of the men were wielding guns and they looked like they knew how to use them.

The men turned and stared in shock at the young boy waving a pole at them. Toby didn't hesitate.

"Take that!" he screamed as he lunged at the one nearest him, striking out with the hook and cracking the man violently across the top of his skull. The huge raider crumpled slowly to the floor with a quiet moan. Before Toby could raise his pole to attack the next one, someone cannoned into him and smacked him heavily to the hard floor of the cabin. The last thing Toby heard was the concerned voice of his dad ringing in his ears.

"Toby? Toby? What have you done to him, you yobs?"

It was some time later when Toby started to come to. His head throbbed, and through the misty fog of pain he was aware of one of the raiders standing over him. The man called out: "Is there any point in taking this one? He looks at death's door. Must have hit his head hard. Does the General want damaged goods?"

"Aye! Chuck him into the inflatable along with the others. If he looks a goner we'll throw him overboard," called back another.

Toby was aware of being lifted clumsily, carried out of the cabin into the cold air and then thrown into empty space. He gasped as he flew through the air and hit the wooden planking on the bottom of the inflatable. As he lay, unable to open his eyes, he heard his dad murmuring to Sylvie nearby. He could smell the metallic tang of blood somewhere. He tried to put his hands to his head, which felt wet and sticky, but they were tied together. A boot nudged him sharply in the ribs.

"Leave my brother alone!" Sylvie squealed.

"Tell your kid to shut up or else she'll end up like her big brother," a voice commanded.

"Don't you touch a hair on her head!" yelled back his dad. This was followed by bursts of laughter from the four men.

"Like you can do anything about it, eh?" said the same man. Toby could hear a tone of authority in this voice and wondered if he was the "Captain" the men referred to. "Now you tell your kids to behave," the man continued, "and we'll all get along just fine. It's not in our interest to knock you about – we want you to arrive in one piece otherwise you'll not be much use to us."

"Aye," another voice cried out, "otherwise it'll be us that'll get it in the neck from the General!"

"Shut up, Calvert! Else I'll have to shut you up, too!" barked the Captain.

Toby lapsed in and out of the darkness of unconsciousness as the inflatable's outboard motor roared into life and the boat took off, bouncing over the waves. He could feel his dad's hand grasping roughly onto his arm, and as he peered painfully into the light, he saw his dad and Sylvie crouching in the bottom of the boat next to him.

Where are they taking us? Toby gritted his teeth as the boat hurtled along, banging violently against the waves and sending spasms of pain ripping through his body.

"You'll like it at Fort George," bawled the Captain, as if reading Toby's thoughts. "We've collected quite a number of folks just like you – loners struggling for an existence in this mad bad world. You'll thank us for rescuing you from your pitiful life. At least you'll have company!"

"What do you want with us?" his dad roared back over the drone of the engine. The men laughed again.

"That'll be a surprise for you to look forward to!" replied one of the men.

"Aye, not a nice one though!" retorted another.

"Calvert! Thought I told you to keep it shut!" commanded the Captain. "We don't want to frighten our guests, do we?" There was a murmur of amusement.

Surprise? What could they mean? It doesn't sound good. I've got to do something quickly. I can't just let them take us to this place, "Fort George". What if they want to eat us? Toby had heard stories of people being eaten but at the time he hadn't believed them. Now... He tried to put all horrible images out of his mind.

I've got to get off this inflatable and back to the Lucky Lady. *That's the best chance we've got. Then I'll be able to follow them in her and rescue Dad and Sylvie from this Fort George.*

As he lay going over his plan in his head, Toby knew that the chances of him getting away and then rescuing his dad and Sylvie were slim. The future looked very bleak but he had to do something. He couldn't just lie here letting these men take them nearer and nearer to what sounded like a death sentence.

He wriggled his toes as the feeling returned to his legs and arms. He peered from under his blood-soaked fringe and saw the men sitting up at the front of the inflatable, scanning the horizon. The boat appeared to be following the craggy cliffs and rocky shores of the Moray coast. Toby knew vaguely where they were. When he had gone down into his den to sleep, his dad had been steering the boat towards Fraserburgh, where they had last seen their friends Jamie and Katie McTavish.

I told Dad not to let the McTavishes go off on their own! He wouldn't listen! I knew something dreadful would happen if we split up. Why won't he ever listen to me?

But this was not the time to go over old hurts and grudges. This was the time for action.

Here goes!

Toby gathered up all his strength and courage and lifted himself bodily from the bottom of the inflatable in one swift leap. Without pausing to look over the side, he flung himself into the churning white waters as the boat sped on.

"TOBY!" he heard his dad scream, before the shock of the cold North Sea hit the breath from his body.

Mustn't gasp! Don't open your mouth! He told himself, as the freezing foaming waves closed over his head. He remembered his dad telling him that most people who went overboard were killed by the cold. The shock of hitting the freezing water made them hyperventilate so that they gasped and swallowed great lungfuls of salty water. Then they drowned. Toby was not going to let that happen to him.

As he dropped down and down into the blackness of the ocean he could hear the dull throbbing of the inflatable's outboard motor vibrating somewhere above his head. He let himself plummet down, keeping his legs together and his arms still. He knew he had to get far enough away from the boat to make the raiders think he had drowned.

As Toby descended, the sea became quieter and quieter and darker and darker. The clear blueness soon turned to menacing black as he struggled to see in front of him.

Got to get these ties off my hands – got to start striking for the surface soon. Don't know how much longer I can hold my breath.

As the dark closed around him, Toby tried not to think of what else might be swimming through the gloom towards him. Something brushed against his legs and then something else darted past his face.

Don't think – just swim!

Toby pulled his hands hard apart in an effort to break the ties but they were fastened tight.

Got to get my hands free. NOW!

Through the ghostly murk he could just make out a large silver object coming towards him fast.

What's that?

2. All Alone in the World

Toby kicked hard with both his legs. His body started to rise upwards as the silver object glided silently underneath him, brushing his feet. Trying not to think what it might be, he strained with all his might against the slippery plastic rope binding his hands. He knew he had to get out of the icy water quickly before he died from the cold.

Got to get to land! Come on, Toby! SWIM!

The rope was cutting deep into the soft skin of his wrists when he tugged his hands through the knots. Steeling himself to the pain, he managed to pull one hand free and struck out sideways, not wanting to surface near to the raiders' boat. Toby swam strongly upwards, silently thanking his dad for dragging him to swimming lessons every Saturday in the years before the red fever. As he neared the surface, the darkness receded and a pale light suffused the water. His sodden clothes were sapping his strength and dragging him down but he kept on pushing and kicking. Finally, he broke through the cresting waves.

Gasping painfully for air, Toby bobbed in the wild waves near the shore, treading water while he took his bearings. Swivelling round he could make out the low grey form of the inflatable as it powered away round the edge of the cliffs dipping into the sea. At the back he glimpsed the anxious silhouette of his dad, scanning the ocean, looking for his son. The raiders had obviously decided not to stop and search for him but, assuming he had drowned, had kept on towards Fort George.

Turning around the other way, Toby was shocked to see the *Lucky Lady* only about a hundred metres away. She was drifting slowly but surely towards the nearby jagged black rocks that guarded the shore.

"*Lady!*" Toby called out as if he could call her to him like he would a dog. The raiders had cut her loose and left her to shipwreck. Her timbers would break up like matchsticks on the unforgiving boulders.

Toby lunged forward, throwing himself through the breaking waves crashing noisily onto the rocks and shore. Reverberating in his ears was the loud gurgle and burble of the pebbles on the beach being pushed backwards and forwards by the water.

Got to get to her before she reaches the rocks! She'll be smashed to smithereens!

Hastily, he pulled off his heavy water-soaked jacket, which disappeared quickly in the foaming water. As he battled towards *Lady*, the small boat was being thrown this way and that like a piece of flotsam in the tide. He hesitated as he gained ground; if he got too close at the wrong time he risked being caught between the boat and the sharp pointy fingers of the rocks. That would be certain death.

Toby swam around to the back of the *Lucky Lady* as she rose and fell with the swell of the waves.

Going to have to time it right – need to jump on just as the back reaches the bottom of the wave. Got to concentrate! I might only have one chance.

Toby bobbed behind the boat for a few seconds, desperately trying not to be picked up and thrown against it by the pounding sea. As he rose and fell he counted, *One elephant, two elephants, three elephants...*

On 'four elephants', he let the wave carry him up against the stern of the boat and, grabbing hold of a ledge, he flung himself over onto the deck. Hardly waiting to catch breath, he raced forward to the wheelhouse. He had to get the engine started and try to power the *Lucky Lady* away from the jaws of death. *Hurry!*

He scrabbled to turn the key with his shaking hand. As the key flicked over, Toby tried to listen for the low rumble of the engine but all he heard was the crashing of the waves all around him.

"Come on *Lady*! Please start!" he begged the boat.

Was there something else he had to do? He had sailed *Lady* a dozen times on his own, but now with fear gripping him, he couldn't think straight. Was there a button to press too? He swept the console with his pale trembling fingers, coming to light on a large red button.

Stupid me! The ignition just primes the engine. I need to press the start button too!

He stabbed at it.

There was a low rumble and a splutter and then the boat's engine jumped into life with a loud roar, churning white foam from the back. Pulling hard on the steering wheel, Toby swung the bow round and pushed up the throttle. The *Lucky Lady* plunged out of the clutches of the incoming tide and pulled clear of the rocks, narrowly missing the sharp teeth of a protruding boulder. Toby braced himself as he wrenched the wheel over, his forearms catching against the hard wood.

Ouch! That hurts!

He noticed for the first time that his wrists were red raw and bloody where he had pulled off the nylon rope.

No time to worry about that now. Got to get after those raiders before they get the chance to hurt Dad and Sylvie. Got to find Fort George!

Toby's teeth chattered with the bone-gnawing cold that clenched him in its grip. He peeled off his wet clothes with one hand while steering with the other. Hung on the back of the door was an old thermal boiler suit his dad had worn when he had worked on an oil platform. Toby snuggled into its warm folds and pulled up the zip. Then he tried to think where Fort George was. Still with one hand on the wheel, he rummaged through his dad's maps with his free hand, pulling them off the map table next to the control panel.

This should be the right map: "The North-East Coast of Scotland". Now where's Fraserburgh? We must have been near there when we were boarded.

Toby soon prodded his finger on the dot marked Fraserburgh, and then traced it upwards following the raiders' route. *I'll have to keep near the coastline so they can't see me. But where is Fort George?* He squinted at the squiggly lines and hundreds of inlets on the map, trying to keep the boat steady. *Yes! There it is – Fort George! It's not far from Inverness.*

Toby reckoned it was sixty to eighty miles from his possible position. Sailing at a speed of ten knots it would take him six to eight hours to get there. But how long would it take the raiders? Their boat was much faster than the *Lucky Lady*, and they probably wouldn't have to stop to look for fuel on the way. He checked *Lady*'s fuel gauge. It read almost full; the raiders hadn't stolen the fuel. They seemed to be interested in only one thing: kidnapping him and his family. *Why?*

Toby, tired and aching, tried to shut his mind off from any bad thoughts and concentrate on steering around the jutting headlands. He placed the map next to him on the control panel along with his dad's old brass telescope, so he could watch for any landmarks that were on the map.

As the small fishing boat motored bravely through the waves, he tried to think of good things, like seeing Sylvie again. He wondered if she had taken Henry, her pet rabbit, with her. Maybe she'd had time to smuggle him inside her fleece pocket? He smiled: the cute fluffy rabbit always cheered her up even when she was terribly poorly.

The spray from the rising waves was lashing the windscreen and Toby fumbled to find the wiper switch. Thud, thud, thud they beat rhythmically while he struggled to bind his bleeding wrists with a ripped-up old hankie. He jumped as something outside clattered and banged in the strengthening wind.

Great! That's all I need – a gale-force wind.

Toby peered out through the rain now lashing onto the deck. Should he keep going in a storm? *Lady* wasn't designed to cope with the winter storms of the North Sea. It might be wise to get her into an inlet where she wouldn't get buffeted by the worst of the weather.

What shall I do? If I keep going I risk losing the boat, but if I put her into shelter I'll lose time and risk losing Dad and Sylvie. I wish Dad was here to decide.

As the boat pitched and rolled onwards, Toby rubbed his aching head with his battered and sore hand. There was nothing for it, he decided, but to keep going to Fort George as long as he could. The storm might blow itself out, and the weather might improve the further north he travelled.

On one rocky outcrop he spied an ancient castle lying in ruins, poised high above the sandy shore. Where once windows had been, now empty black holes looked out over the sea.

That would be an excellent place for a lookout. You could see for miles over land and sea from there.

The castle looked vaguely familiar but he had never seen it from the sea. Before the red fever, when they had had a normal life of family outings and picnics, his mum and dad used to take them to a castle somewhere along this bit of coast.

It had been called Find... Finhorn? No – was it Findochty? No, it was Findlater Castle. I remember now. This must be it! Yes – there it is on the map.

They had walked to it from a car park in a farmyard, scrambling down the grassy bank to cross the narrow path to the castle. Mum would shout out "Watch where you're going!" and "Be careful!" as he and his dad climbed up and around the crumbling walls of the ruin. Afterwards they would take a picnic down to the beach below and play with their dog, Monty, throwing sticks into the waves for him to swim after.

Toby's tummy rumbled as he remembered the delicious fish and chips they ate for tea in the nearby fishing village of Portsoy. His mum loved the gift shop there and always bought a smooth coloured egg, crafted from the local marble, to add to her collection. Toby wondered where those eggs were now.

Don't look back! Those days are gone forever.

He glanced to the castle and something caught his eye. A flickering shadow passed across one of the gaping holes. He tensed and then strained to see what it was. Nothing moved.

Must have been imagining it.

But then again, a quick movement attracted his attention. Dark shadows flitted across an open stone doorway.

"NO! Not the dogs! Not here!" Toby shouted out. The black head of a large dog appeared in a doorway. This was no ordinary mongrel, no pet dog roaming loose after losing its owner to the red fever. This was a huge powerful dog that knew how to hunt in packs. It would not be on its own. Toby watched nervously for more of them. Sure enough, within a few seconds three dogs were looking out of the doorway. They sniffed the air and turned to look out to sea.

They've seen me! Thank goodness I'm too far away for them to swim out to me. But Toby still felt a cold fear clutching at his insides. He hated the dogs. They were the reason why he and his dad and Sylvie had had to leave their lighthouse home on the edge of the sea at Collieston. They were the reason why it had become unsafe to travel freely on land, and they were the reason why his mum was no longer with them.

Don't worry about that now! I'm no use to Dad and Sylvie if I get scared. Be strong!

More dark shadows passed the windows and another three dogs joined the others at the doorway. Toby frowned; there seemed to be a lot of dogs for such a remote place. It was almost as if they had been following him.

Stop thinking, you idiot! Get on and decide what you're going to do when you get to Fort George.

But no matter how hard he tried to plan, Toby didn't have a clue what he was going to do. He didn't know what he was going to find when he got there.

The weather did improve as the *Lucky Lady* chugged along the coast. He could see from the map that Fort George stood on a promontory jutting out into the inlet of the Moray Firth, which led to Inverness. As long as he followed the coastline he couldn't go wrong, unless a misty haar descended.

The wintry sun flickered on the waves as he steered the boat westwards. Toby became aware of the dappled purple and green hills to his right at he sailed further into the Firth.

That must be the Black Isle.

He began to swing the boat slowly out into the middle of the estuary to save fuel. The flow of the tide was faster here, and the *Lucky Lady* sped forwards. Before long he spotted a piece of land jutting out and the estuary narrowed. He would be too visible sailing into water so close to the land. He decided to find a place to anchor up and wait for the cover of darkness.

Will I find the fort in the dark? Will I find Dad and Sylvie in the dark? Be positive! I can do this. I know I can. I have to.

3. A Mighty Fort

As darkness crept slowly over the hills, Toby edged the *Lucky Lady* closer and closer to the headland upon which stood Fort George.

"What on earth?" he gasped. An enormous wall of grey stone towered high above him, sweeping sideways as far as he could see. Toby had never seen such an awesome structure. Whoever had built it had been serious about keeping out invaders. High up, sited at intervals on the top of the wall, he could just make out a line of small, round stone buildings. Each had a fancy roof with a stone ball sat on top, and each had several slits in the walls to give anyone occupying them an excellent view of the sea.

Sentry posts and lots of them. Better be careful. Someone might be watching out right now.

Toby couldn't see any lights shining from the sentry towers but that didn't mean someone wasn't keeping guard.

He searched desperately for a pier where he could tie up the *Lucky Lady*. The dinghy that was usually moored to the back of the boat had been lost in the raiders' attack. The only other choice was to anchor the *Lady* and swim in the icy water to the shore. As the wintry evening closed in, he didn't like that idea at all.

One cold dunking in a day was quite enough.

Toby cut the engine to a quiet purr and steered cautiously round the headland to his left. He peered up into the gloom of the lowering sky.

He tried not to think about what he was going to do once he got into Fort George, even if, indeed, he *could* get into it. The place looked totally impenetrable.

On this side of the fort, the beach was protected with large wooden poles dug into the shingle. Their stark angular forms threw eerie shadows across the water.

Must have been put there to stop invaders storming the beach.

Holding his breath, he steered round the end of the headland and saw something that gladdened his heart. Built into the side of the headland was a small stone harbour. The water was deeper here and Toby easily manoeuvred the *Lucky Lady* through the harbour opening, and bumped her up alongside a wall.

This is the tricky part. He clutched *Lady*'s rope and leapt from the moving boat up onto the wall. Pulling the rope tight behind him, he quickly wound it around a bollard on the quayside. *Lady* came to a bobbing halt.

Phew!

Toby glanced around him. There was no sign of anybody or anything, only the sound of the roaring wind as it whipped across the sea with a vengeful bitterness. He shivered with the cold but also with dread of what might lie ahead. He tugged the zipper on the boiler suit right up to his chin and pulled down his black woolly hat.

Better move fast just in case there is someone around.

He slunk low to the ground and half ran, half hopped into the lee of the tall walls, which seemed to bristle with ferocity and history.

Bet you've seen some scary sights. Toby clung against the chilly damp stones. He stared through the growing dark up to his left where a track led through an archway into the fort. He then spotted the inflatable lying beached on the shingle shore like a fat grey whale. He ran up to it and felt the outboard motor. It was still warm; the raiders couldn't have arrived long before him. Then he had a brilliant idea. Reaching into his pocket to pull out his Swiss Army knife, he unsheathed the biggest blade and sank it deep into the side of the plastic boat. With a soft hiss the air escaped. Toby punched the boat in several more places with his knife.

We don't want them chasing us when we escape. When we escape? More like if *we escape!*

He scraped along the wall and then dropped down onto the track where it disappeared into an entrance. A massive wooden door studded with black nuts and bolts stood in front of him.

"Oh no! No way am I going to get through that!" he blurted out aloud, and then could have kicked himself for being so stupid.

Shut UP!

But as Toby looked at the door, he realised that a much smaller door was built inside it, disguised by the pattern of nuts and bolts. He took hold of a particularly large nut and tried to turn it. It slid round to the right and the tiny door swung open.

Yeah! He bent low and stepped through the opening into the fort.

Something hit him hard in the back and he felt the ground rush up to meet him. As a white flash collided with darkness in his head, Toby fell to the ground, unconscious.

When a thin dull light streamed through the barred windows, Toby woke. Every inch of him felt black and blue. He sniffed heavily but was too shocked to cry. So much for his rescue mission. Now it was him who needed rescuing.

He took in his surroundings. He was lying on a narrow metal bed at the end of a row, on top of a thin jute mattress that appeared to be stuffed with straw. Toby could feel the itchy stalks pushing through the coarse cloth.

He rolled over slowly and gasped: there, stood in the corner, was a tall man wearing a large bearskin hat and a caped greatcoat. The man was standing stock-still. The shadows from the low dawn light threw him into relief so that Toby couldn't see his face, nor could he hear his breathing.

Where am I? This looks like an old prison. How long have I been here? And who's that weirdo dressed up as a soldier from who knows when? How am I going to get out with him there?

Toby rolled quietly over to face the other way but there seemed no possibility of escape there either. He felt a heavy weight descend upon him. He had failed his dad and Sylvie at almost the first hurdle. Now he had to lie here and wait for the men, whoever they were, to come and dispose of him however they wanted. No one was going to come and rescue him. No one even knew he was here. It was hopeless.

As if on cue, the door banged open and two men strode into the chamber. Toby flinched as they grabbed him by his raw and throbbing wrists, and hauled him to his feet. The man they called the Captain appeared at the doorway.

"Now young man! Not dead after all, eh? You may well wish you were once we've finished with you."

"What do you want with me and my dad and Sylvie?" Toby blurted out. One of the raiders dug him hard in the ribs.

"Only speak when the Captain says you can!" he growled.

"That's right Calvert, you teach this young pup a few manners," said the Captain. "Now, I want to know a few things about your dad and what he used to do. He's not telling us but I reckon you will."

"Well, you reckoned wrong, didn't you?" Toby cried. The raider gave him a harder thump. Toby felt the man's fist connect with a bruise, and gasped.

"We don't want to hurt you; *we* don't do torture. We leave that to the General. He's strange that way – gets pleasure out of other people's pain," continued the Captain, smiling as he advanced towards Toby. Toby could now see the man clearly: he was smaller than the others, but somehow filled the room with his menacing presence. His dark skin was covered with the white wheals of old scars and, with his short legs and heavy-set body, he reminded Toby of a pit bull terrier he had once seen in Aberdeen. The dog had been a fighter and carried the scars to prove it, just like this man.

"Who's this General? That's a bit sad, isn't it — giving yourselves military ranks?" jeered Toby, trying to sound a lot braver than he felt. "Playing at being soldiers, are you?" He braced himself for what he felt sure the raider was going to do to him. But instead, the Captain stuck his face right up to Toby's and sneeringly said,

"HA! You won't think we're playing at soldiers once you see what we've done at New Caledonia! You'll be amazed when you see what the General has built — a whole new world! Unfortunately for you, though, you are not one of the lucky ones who are going to be able to enjoy what we've created. No, you see you haven't got one of these —"

The Captain pulled back the cuff of his jacket and shoved his arm under Toby's nose. There, tattooed in black and red ink, were the initials,

"And what's more, you are never going to get one!" The Captain laughed. "Only the hand-picked special commandos have this and only *they* will get to reap the benefits of the new country we have built. Yes, we'll live a life of luxury while people like you and your dad will do all the work!"

"You're crazy!" cried Toby, straining away from the Captain's putrid breath.

"Crazy? Don't you think you need to be a bit crazy to survive the mess this world is in?" the Captain spat in Toby's face. Up close, Toby could see the madness in the man's eyes. He was seriously scary.

How worrying is that? If the Captain is this mad – how much madder must this General be?

Just then another raider appeared at the door.

"Boss?" the man called to the Captain. "There's a message just come in from the General. Seems like there's been more trouble at Fort William." Forgetting Toby, the Captain wheeled about and, striding over to the door, struck the man hard across the face with his hand.

"How many times have I told you to address me as 'Captain'? Not 'Boss'!" he screamed. The raider muttered some apology as the Captain pushed past him, leaving the two raiders holding Toby. They threw him roughly back onto the bed and then stormed off after their leader, only pausing to leer at the man in the doorway.

"Yes, Jones, you moron – he's called the Captain! Get it?" said Calvert with a sneer. "Now lock up our little friend here, and make sure you do it properly!"

Seems like these guys are not all soldiers. Maybe I can use that to my advantage?

"What you smiling about?" Jones asked Toby. "You think it's funny? Wait 'til you meet the General!"

"So, have you got one of those tattoos? Are you one of the chosen few?" Toby asked him, thinking that it could be a good idea to try and make Jones a friend. He remembered watching a film a long time ago, about a girl who was kidnapped. She had survived by being friendly with her captors who then saw her as a person and found it difficult to do her any harm.

That feels like a good plan – it's the only one I've got just now.

"Mind your own business!" replied Jones, leaving the prison and slamming the door shut behind him. Toby listened as the locks were turned and bolts drawn.

So much for that plan! Doesn't sound like he's forgotten to bolt the door, either. And he's locked that weirdo in the corner in with me. He didn't have much to say, did he?

Toby glanced over at the motionless figure in the shadows, and then lay down on the prickly bed, clutching his sore stomach, which was now grumbling with hunger. Things couldn't really get much worse – could they? All his plans now seemed totally useless, his energy was spent and his whole body ached.

Where are Dad and Sylvie? They might be in the very next room… If I was to shout they would at least know I was still alive. They must be worried sick. I'll just rest a little while and then try to let them know I'm here.

Toby closed his eyes, tiredness overcame him, and he fell into an exhausted slumber.

4. Wolf-Girl

"Boy! Wake up, boy!" Someone was shaking him hard and hissing into his ear.

"What? Am I dreaming?" Toby mumbled. The short rest had not cured his sore, heavy body.

"Get up and hurry!" The hissing had become much more urgent and the shaking rougher. Toby sat bolt upright and stared at the figure sitting on his bed. The voice had definitely sounded like a girl, but the apparition on the bed looked more like a cross between a wolf and wild Mowgli-child.

"What ARE you?" he asked, more than a little scared.

"Shush! We've got to leave now, boy! Hurry!" The strange wolf-like creature pulled at his hand and turned to go.

"What about him?" Toby hissed back, pointing at the striking figure stood by the window. The soldier was still standing stoically to attention.

"That's a dummy! He was there for the tourists who used to visit here. They had their photos taken with him."

"Of course, I knew it was a dummy. Course I did," Toby said to her back as she scurried away to a far door. "What *is* this place anyway?"

"This is the guardroom. You'd better move fast – they're planning to come back for you soon."

The girl slowly swung the heavy wooden door of the guardroom open and peered out. She slipped through the doorway and disappeared into the grey mistiness outside.

Is this a trap? Should I go with this strange girl?

She looked so weird, and how had she got into the guardroom? Could she walk through locked doors? Maybe she was a figment of his imagination. It could all be a dream. Maybe he was about to wake up to find himself being beaten up by a soldier with an enormous bearskin hat on his head.

Staying here waiting for the men to come back and get me seems like a bad idea.

Toby dragged his aching limbs to the door and, peeking out, saw a huge square of grass. On the other side sat a squat line of Georgian town houses, just like ones Toby had seen on a visit to Edinburgh once with his mum and dad. The grey slate roofs peaked up above creamy mist, which was shot through with blades of sunlight.

This place is weird. It's like a town inside a fortress. Now where's that wolf-girl gone? She might know where Dad and Sylvie are. I've got to find them.

Toby didn't think it a good idea to wander into the middle of the square – he would be too visible. He clung to the walls. Just as he was passing a rusted metal door with GAOL HOUSE painted on it, he heard a noise.

"Psst... in here," the girl's voice called.

Toby ducked in behind the door.

"What are you doing?" he whispered angrily at her.

"We're going to the ravelin and then down into the outworks. Later, we can get out of a sluice gate and onto the beach, then back to your boat."

"Whoa! What are you on about? The ravelin? What's that? And I need to find my dad and my sister. I'm not leaving here without them… And how did you know I came in a boat?" Toby hoped it was his most commanding voice. He wasn't going to take orders from a girl, especially one that looked like a wolf, and smelt like one too.

"Get a grip!" the girl shook his sore arm. "You need to leave now if you want to live. Your family have already been moved to another station. And as for knowing how you arrived – you might as well have put the flags out! I could see you coming for miles."

"Oh," said Toby lamely. Had he really been that useless? "What do you mean 'station'? What is this place?"

"Don't you know anything?" she said crossly. "This is a collecting station – these men —"

"I call them raiders," interrupted Toby.

"Whatever! Call them what you like, but they're evil. Come on – I'll explain later!"

Just then a blood-curdling howl vent the air. It sounded very close.

"The dogs are here?" Toby clutched at the girl's grimy arm.

"What are you talking about?" she looked at him as if he was the mad one. "We must go!"

The girl slinked out of the door again and this time Toby made sure that he was right behind her.

"I'm taking you to somewhere safe just now," she crept along the wall. "This is a good time to move. Most of the men drink at night and are useless by morning."

Toby concentrated on following her closely as she slipped in and out of the shadows. Then they climbed up a grassy rampart, which took them onto the huge broad walls of the fort at the level of the house roofs.

They silently trotted along the top of the wide parapet, carefully keeping to the wall on the seaward side. On the other side the grass fell steeply down a bank to land in the inner yards. They slowed to negotiate a slippery grass rampart that led to a smaller courtyard. In the centre was a large sandy-coloured church. The girl sprinted towards it, leaping over the grass and disappearing into a side porch. Toby followed, tumbling in behind her.

"Wow!" he cried. Inside the church the hazy light streaming through the side windows lit clouds of dust, throwing a smoky aura down the transept. He ran to the end of the aisle and peered up at the stained-glass windows. One had a picture of an angel playing the bagpipes. It was a long time since he had been in a church and he'd forgotten how beautiful and peaceful they were.

"Are we safe here?" he turned to ask the girl.

"Yes, the raiders don't come here. I've made them think it's haunted." Toby could just make out the glimpse of a smile from under her wolf get-up. "And some are scared of facing their God because of the things they have done since the red fever."

Toby followed the girl into the rear of the church where she pulled back a thick brocade curtain. Behind it was a heavy wooden door that she unlocked to reveal a small vestry. Built into the floor was a trapdoor, which the girl lifted to expose a flight of steps going down into the bowels of the church. She signalled Toby to follow. Pulling the door quietly closed behind them, they took the steps down and down into a narrow passageway that smelt of dust and old bones. The staircase was lit by small electric lights that came on when they approached and went off as they passed, leaving the passage behind them in the dark. Toby realised that they were going down into a cave system. The stairs got shallower and the path widened out.

"Amazing!" he exclaimed as he climbed downwards. It was like being in the tunnel in *Alice in Wonderland*. The walls were strung with equipment: reels of pipes and hoses, skeins of rope, anchors, fishing rods and nets, gas cylinders, water carriers, spades and forks, boxes of nails, bundles of wire, a long ladder and even a wheel barrow.

At the end of the steps the tunnel opened out into a large cave, which was lit with coloured fairy lights strung along its wall. This gave it a Christmassy look, like a fairy grotto. The cave was laid out as a living room with proper chairs, a coffee table and even a battered leather settee complete with fluffy cushions. In the corner sat an old TV with a picture of a Santa on his sleigh stuck to the screen. To one side of the cave was a small kitchenette with a sink, cooker and a hot-water boiler. On the other side was a glass water distiller, and at the back of the room sat a huge generator, quietly humming.

"Gosh! I'm impressed," Toby swivelled on his heels to take it all in. "How long did it take you to do all of this?"

The girl was busy fiddling with a gas canister connected to the cooker.

"My father made it. You hungry?" she asked.

Toby sat down on the leather settee and stroked a fluffy cushion that reminded him of Henry, Sylvie's rabbit.

"My name's Toby Tennant, what's yours?"

She turned to stare at him as if he had just landed from outer space. Toby could see her better now and under the soft, coloured lights she looked even weirder than he first thought. Draped over her shoulders was a huge, grizzled grey wolf skin that hung way down past her knees. It was complete with the head of the wolf, which perched on top of her head. The whole thing was attached to her body at various places with old baler twine. Toby wondered whether this was where the smell came from: the skin looked moth-eaten and mangy. The wolf's head had been stuffed so that the yellowing fangs gaped open in a vicious snarl and the beady glass eyes stared at him in animosity. The girl untied the skin cloak and, lifting the wolf's sneering face from hers, hung the whole thing up on a coat stand.

"My name is Natasha Marie Anya Gablinski, but my mates call me Tash — I mean, my mates used to call me Tash; I don't have any now." She expertly lit the gas stove, and placed a pan on the hob.

"Me neither. Well, I do have Jamie, but I don't know where he is right now..." Toby muttered. "Can I help?"

"No, thanks. I can take of everything myself. I'm going to cook us some food."

"Ok," Toby wondered at the slightly stilted way she spoke. Maybe she hadn't spoken to anyone for ages and had forgotten how. He watched her opening some tins and packets and mixing stuff up in the pan. She could be about his age. She was slight but athletic. Her face was smeared with black gunge, presumably for camouflage, but beneath it Toby could make out a rich amber skin tone, which showed off her very white teeth.

Wonder how she keeps her teeth so nice? Toby self-consciously rubbed his with the cuff of his grimy boiler suit. He couldn't remember when he had last given them a good brush. Since his mum was no longer around to remind him, he'd given up.

"How did you get me out of that guardroom? It must have been locked," he asked. Tash jangled a bunch of keys that were tied to a belt on her waist.

"My great-grandmamma was in France during World War Two, and was in the freedom fighters – the Resistance. They gave her these skeleton keys. They're very old so they only work on old locks."

"Wow! What an exciting great-grandma! I think mine spent the war knitting socks for the army."

"Mine was very brave, and these keys are very handy."

"So how do you know my dad and sister have been moved already? Have you seen them? Are they ok? The raiders haven't hurt them, have they?" Toby asked. As he blurted out his fears, it was like opening the floodgates of his emotions. He started to sob – great big wrenching sobs tearing a pain in his chest. He'd been bottling everything up inside and, now that he felt safe, it was all coming out.

Must be that whack I got on my head. It's turned me into a gibbering wreck! What must she think of me?

5. In the Wolf's Lair

Tash said nothing. She left the cooker and came over and sat beside him. Taking his scarred filthy hand into her small brown one, she sat quietly and held it until he had cried himself out. Then she reached over to the coffee table and passed him a big box of soft tissues. Toby took a handful and blew his nose noisily.

"Thanks," he blubbered, sniffing hard. "I'm so sorry."

"You've no need to be sorry," said Tash, returning his hand to him. Toby felt a small pang of disappointment as she did so. It had been comforting. His mum had always held his hand at bad times.

"Where have the raiders taken my family? And who is this General they're all frightened of?" Toby asked, trying to regain his composure while dabbing at his red nose and bleary eyes. Tash returned to her cooking.

"Late last night the men came back from a hunting trip —"

"Hunting trip? Is that what they call kidnapping poor frightened families?"

"Yes, the men like to go on their hunting trips. I hear them talking about their forays up and down the coast. I can wander quite freely around the fort in the dark, camouflaged in my wolf skin. I can get up close, if I hide in the shadows, and listen to them bragging about who they caught and what they did to them."

"*What?*" yelled Toby, jumping up. "I don't know if I can hear any more."

"Your dad and little sister are ok, though. I heard the men saying that the General wanted to see them. I have never seen him here but I know he is a very scary person and will stop at nothing to get his own way. Seems he's particularly interested in your dad for some reason. Is your dad a doctor? Or a scientist?" asked Tash.

"No, he's a... well, he *was* an engineer. He used to work in the oil industry before the red fever came. But the raiders told me Dad wouldn't tell them what he used to do. He's brave, is my dad. He wouldn't want to help them in any way. They wanted me to tell them but I wouldn't."

"Anyhow, they've taken your dad and sister to see the General – they left early this morning in one of the vans."

"Where is this General?"

"I don't know," she calmly replied, stirring the pan.

Toby sat down abruptly and held his throbbing head in his hands, tearing at his hair.

"Oh! This gets worse and worse. What could the General want with my dad and Sylvie?"

"Pretty name, 'Sylvie'," mused Tash, as she poured her concoction out into two large, chipped bowls. She motioned to Toby to sit down at the kitchen table. "I wish I knew why these bad men are kidnapping people. They've taken my father and mother, also."

Oh no, she must feel desperate about that too. Funny – she seems very calm.

Toby went to the table and sat down. The tomatoey stew of pasta and chunky chicken pieces smelt delicious. But he was distracted even through his hunger. Why didn't Tash seem more bothered if the raiders had her mum and dad?

"Don't you want to find your parents?" he asked. Tash pointed to his spoon and fork.

"Eat," she commanded. "You'll feel better for it." He was too ravenous to argue. They ate in silence and it wasn't until the last drop of stew had been gulped down that Tash looked up and spoke. "My father told me to stay here. He said I was not to go looking for him and mother if they ever got taken. They got taken three months ago. We were living in the fort then, but these raiders, as you call them, broke in one night and took everybody. I was lucky: my father sent me down here and here I have stayed."

She got up from the table to clear the bowls and came back with a tub of warm water, a bottle of disinfectant and a roll of cotton wool. "Here," she said, "you have a cut on the back of your head. You'd better wash it before it gets infected."

Toby winced as he sponged the cut gingerly with the cotton doused in disinfectant.

"Were there many people living here in the fort?" he asked, grimacing.

"Yes, about forty: four families and some others. Me and Father and Mother have lived here since the red fever came. My father is very clever. He told the others to make a cave so that if bad men came we could all hide. But the others said that they were safe in Fort George; they thought that nobody could get in. But the bad men did."

"Your dad was right. There's very little that'll stop those raiders, unfortunately. And the dogs are just as bad," said Toby.

"What is it with you and dogs? We've had no problems here with dogs. We used to have collies for working our sheep, but the raiders took them, along with the sheep."

"Well," said Toby, "that howl we heard was no ordinary dog. I saw some big dogs on the coast, at a place called Findlater Castle. I could have sworn they were following me."

"Why would they do that?" asked Tash.

"Maybe they think I will lead them to more humans, and where there are humans, there's food."

"Aren't you assuming a bit much of these dogs? I mean, dogs thinking ahead, dogs having a plan – that sounds a bit weird to me."

As they sat in the safety of Tash's home, under the coloured fairy lights, Toby recounted his story of the dogs. He told how his friend, Jamie, and Jamie's mum, Katie, who was a scientist, had been studying them in Aberdeen. Katie had come to the conclusion that the dogs there had been infected with the rcd fever. But instead of making them ill and die like it did most of the humans, it mutated their genes so that they were evolving at a much faster rate. They were growing into bigger, cleverer animals.

Toby had seen with his own eyes how one large, ferocious dog was acting as their leader. This dog seemed to have a plan. Jamie and his mum called this pack leader "Cerberus", after the three-headed dog in Greek mythology that guards the mouth of hell.

"He sounds like a clever animal. Dogs don't usually plan," observed Tash.

"Yes. We don't know what his plan is," said Toby. "I can probably guess though: total domination of Scotland if not the whole country. Those dogs I saw on the way here are probably scouting ahead. The others may not be far behind. That howl was probably one of them, telling the others."

"Telling?" Tash was sceptical.

"Yes, they're really good at communicating. That howl would have been calling them here. They'll know now that this fort is a human settlement. By coming here I've led them to it."

"Sorry, Toby," said Tash, "this all sounds a little... far-fetched?"

"I know it must seem crazy. But this is a crazy world now – a world where *you* have to wear a wolf cape. Where did you get that? Is it real?"

"Yes. It belonged to my father. He gave it to me before he left." She looked downcast at this memory, so Toby changed the subject.

"Are you Scottish? You don't sound it."

"Yes, I was born in Inverness, but my parents are from many places. My mother is Russian, and Father is from Poland, though they have both lived all over the world. They speak many languages, but their English is not so good, so mine isn't either. I know lots about different cultures, though."

"That's brilliant – you must have things in your head I can't even imagine. I think you'll get on well with Jamie, my pal: he loves learning stuff." The thought of Jamie brought Toby back to earth with a bump. He missed his friend.

I wonder where he is? I hope his mum's ok, too, and Belle. Toby was about to tell Tash the story of how he and his dad on the *Lucky Lady* had rescued Jamie and his big white dog, Belle. But glancing over the table, he saw that she had fallen fast asleep, with her head on her hands.

"Sleep well, strange girl," he whispered, then went and lay down on the settee. Cuddling the Henry-like cushion to his chest, Toby, too, was asleep in seconds. But his dreams were plagued by dogs: big black dogs chasing him over the rooftops of Fort George. As fast as he ran, the dogs could run faster, and soon they had him pinned up against the church door. He dodged them and sped into the church, but they followed him. Under the stained-glass windows he stood face to face with a massive black dog that had a stub for a tail. This could only be Cerberus. As Toby prayed to the angel playing the bagpipes to save him, Cerberus opened his great, slavering jaws, lifted his head and let out an ear-bursting howl, shaking the very foundations of the church:

HOOOOOOOOOOOOOOOOOOOOOOOOWL!

Toby jumped awake with a sickening jolt. He was drenched in sweat, and shaking.

Was that just in his dream? Or had he really heard the howl of Cerberus?

6. Under Attack

"Did you hear that?" Toby exclaimed, shaking Tash by the arm. "Wake up! We need to go and see if the dogs are here!"

Tash lifted her tousled head from the table and yawned.

"We're safe here. No dogs can get into Fort George. It's impossible, don't worry."

"You don't know these dogs like I do. They can do loads of stuff normal mutts wouldn't even think about. Please, Tash, we must go and see. Listen: you won't be able to stay here if the dogs take over Fort George. They're not like the raiders that you can duck and dive from," Toby babbled. "Dogs can smell you and they will hunt you down. Even if they didn't get in here, you'd never be able to leave again. Do you want to live the rest of your life in this cave?"

Toby was going to add something about Tash rescuing her family – didn't she think she should at least make some effort to find out where they had been taken? – but then he thought that was probably going too far. As far as Tash was concerned she was just obeying her father's orders, and she saw nothing wrong in that. Toby, on the other hand, was determined to find out where his dad and Sylvie were and mount a rescue mission.

But first he had to find out what was happening outside. If the dogs were here, that might change all of their plans.

"Let's get out of here," he said in an authoritative voice, pulling on his jacket. Tash glanced at him and he saw in her eyes she'd realised there was no persuading him otherwise.

"Ok." She pulled on the wolf skin.

"Where's the best place to watch the land side of the fort?"

"The ravelin," said Tash. "It's a high area outside the main wall, but it's dangerous to get to. We must go through the main door and cross the main bridge. It won't be easy – the raiders will be looking for you."

"We'll manage. How about we go right round the outside of the fort instead?"

"Ok, I'll show you how. Come on."

Tash picked up a torch in the living room, and led Toby into a cave at the back. Hidden in this cave was another trapdoor, this time in the ceiling, which opened into a set of rough-hewn steps carved out of the rock. These took them up and up until they came to another hatchway. Climbing through, Toby found himself standing on the shore at the very end of the headland that poked out into the sea. The fort walls towered up behind him.

Did I really hear a dog? Was it just my overactive imagination playing tricks on me?

All he could hear now was the constant noise of the waves breaking and crackling on the shingle. He could see that they had been asleep for most of the day and the sun was now low in the sky. The light had a magical quality: it was bright and brittle and bounced off the hard surfaces of the fort like spears in battle.

"When does it get dark up here?" he asked Tash. Toby knew that as you moved north the hours of daylight grew less in winter, and more in summer. He remembered his dad telling him that up north on Orkney you could read a book outside at midnight in summer. Tash checked her watch.

"Soon."

Toby felt a strange dread coming over him. If the dogs were going to attack Fort George, the best time would be at night when they'd be hard to see – their black coats would merge into the dark.

"Ok, which is the shortest route to the ravelin?" he asked Tash. She hesitated, so he decided to go left, which would take him past the little harbour in which, hopefully, the *Lucky Lady* still sat. This way he could check whether she was ready to go; they might need her soon.

Toby and Tash made their way swiftly along the outside wall of the fort, keeping in its shadows. They passed the harbour where the *Lucky Lady* still bobbed along the quayside. Toby breathed a sigh of relief, but this soon turned to dismay when he saw that moored nearby was a silver, streamlined motor boat.

"You ever seen that before?" he pointed at the sleek vessel.

"No, but sometimes other men come to swap people for food. The raiders always seem to have lots of food. These men that come are really bad – more like pirates."

"I don't think I want to hear any more."

This is hopeless. I'm really up against it, what with pirates and *raiders! All I need now is for the dogs to appear...*

As if on cue, a spine-chilling howl echoed across the spit of sand and shingle. Toby felt every hair on the back of his neck stand up with fear and dread.

"Oh no!" he gasped. There could be no mistaking that sound.

"I heard it this time," Tash whispered hastily.

"I wonder where it's coming from? Come on, let's get to the ravelin."

They broke into a run and raced across a disused car park where a couple of old cars lay rusting in the salty air. They weren't bothering to keep to the walls anymore; getting back inside the fort was the priority. Toby felt his bruises and sprains begin to complain, but then the adrenalin kicked in. He grabbed Tash's hand and together they sprinted over the grass and towards an angled corner of the wall that stuck out into the sea.

"Here!" panted Tash. "Here's the sluice gate!" Toby slowed to a halt and ran his hands frantically over the cold wet stones of the outer wall. Panic took hold of him, and it was as if he could feel the very claws of Cerberus scratching his back.

"Hush," said Tash quietly. She calmly ran her hand over the lower base of the wall, then gave a tug on a metal lever. A small wooden door in the bottom of a larger, metal-banded sluice gate swung open. "In here."

It was like going into another world. Inside, the walls seemed even higher; they were stood in a vast dry moat between the inner and the outer parapets of the fort. Underfoot was deep, lush green grass.

Tash ran to the right of the moat with Toby following close behind. In the growing dusk they could just make out a gleaming white wooden bridge above them. It spanned the moat from the fort to a high piece of ground that was the ravelin. Tash swung right, and started to climb up a steep path, gripping onto tall, spiky grass for handholds.

When they reached the top, where two metal gates flanked the bridge, they were both out of breath. They stopped and took in their surroundings as the chill winter air bit through their clothes. Toby tried not to let Tash see him shiver.

"Wait," he said, "let's take a look and see if we can spot any dogs. There's a great view from here." He sprinted to a far wall, legged up it and onto the top. Even in the dusky gloom of the late winter's afternoon, he could see for miles across the vast green bank that lay to the landward side in front of the fort. Before the bank reached the fort, there was a series of deep ditches lined with sharp-pointed stakes.

"Who built this place and what for?" he asked Tash. "It's amazing. Look at how deep those ditches are, and look how well fortified the entrance is..." Just then, something moved in the corner of his vision. He dropped to the ground like a stone.

"What is it? Toby?" asked Tash anxiously.

Toby put his finger to his lips, and pointed out across the huge bank into the distance. "I saw something moving out there."

"You sure? Not flying haggis perhaps?" she smiled,

making it obvious she thought he was a bit deranged and needed humouring.

"No, I saw something that looked like a dog. I'm sure of it," he replied crossly, turning to face her. She smiled again, but then her face changed as she looked over his shoulder out towards the grassy area.

"Toby, you did see a dog," she said slowly, her eyes widening in fright. "Oh, Toby! There are hundreds of them!"

Toby swung around and followed her gaze. There were hundreds of dark shadows slinking over the vast greenness of the bank: dogs trotting calmly and purposefully in pairs, side by side. They were all big and black or brown. And they were coming towards the fort.

"We need to get away from here NOW!" Toby shrieked at Tash. He grabbed her arm, pulling her towards the wooden bridge over the moat.

"Toby, it's safe here." But Toby felt a thread of panic winding itself around his innards. He knew what these dogs were capable of: they could work out gates and catches, open doors and jump great heights to get where they wanted. Nowhere was safe.

He took one last look across the grass and the undulating sea of dogs. Then he spotted him. There, out in front, was one that looked bigger and blacker than the rest. Toby could see the stumpy tail: it was Cerberus. The dog stopped, and the others came to a halt behind him. Cerberus lifted his head, sniffed the evening air, and let out an almighty howl that made Toby's stomach curl up into a cold hard knot.

Oh no! This is my worst nightmare come true.

7. Surrender?

Toby's feet felt like they were nailed to the ground. The cold fear from seeing Cerberus had numbed his mind. It was like being in one of Sylvie's nightmares where Cerberus was about to attack her with his large slavering jaws drooling and she had screamed out to his dad in her sleep and —

"Toby!" screamed Tash. "Run!" She rushed back to where he stood rooted to the spot and slapped him hard across his face.

"Ouch! That hurt!" Toby cried, but the stinging pain brought him back to his senses. He sprinted after her, heading back towards the white wooden bridge. Too late. The raiders were already there. Four of them were standing on the bridge, guns braced to their shoulders, poised to fire.

"Look out!" shouted Toby, ducking down out of sight, but the raiders had seen him.

"It's the kid!" one of them yelled. "He's with a dog! Or is it a wolf?"

"He must have brought the dogs with him!" another yelled back. "He must have led them here to attack us! Shoot him!"

"No!" cried out another, "the General doesn't want a dead kid! Orders are to bring him back alive, remember? Just shoot at the dogs to frighten them off, but don't waste any ammo!"

Toby recognised the voice of the Captain giving the orders. He and Tash were now trapped on the ravelin, an isolated island sticking up in the outer defences of the fort. In one direction the raiders stood on the bridge, and in the other direction a sea of dogs was running towards him. The dogs would have to cross the line of sharpened fir trees, leap over deep ditches *and* scale the enormous stone wall. Toby didn't think even Cerberus was big and brave enough for that, especially if the raiders started shooting.

He hid behind a guardhouse, and tried to think what to do next. Would the raiders come and grab him now? Or would they defend the fort from the dogs first?

Think! Quickly – there must be another way off here and back into the moat. Perhaps I can get there before the dogs do. And where is Tash?

Tash seemed to have vanished into thin air. Toby couldn't see any sign of the grey wolf-girl anywhere. He felt a stab of anger at her for leaving him on his own as soon as trouble kicked off.

Can't blame her I suppose – it's about survival of the fittest. That's why she's survived so long here on her own against the raiders: she's brilliant at merging in, disappearing, becoming part of the fort... Great idea! That's what I need to do. Thanks, Tash.

Toby looked around him. There was a large greasy puddle to his right. He grimaced and stuck his hands into it. It was cold and slimy and smelt of putrefying pig muck. Holding his nose with one hand, he scooped up a handful and smeared it over his face and neck, feeling the yucky gunge oozing down his chest. Then he rubbed it over his faded green boiler suit. Now he looked like something that had crawled out of a toxic lagoon in a horror film.

There must be another way off here. I'll try to the left – we haven't been to that side of the ravelin.

Lying low and poking his head out slowly, Toby noticed a worn path that led from the main bridge round past the guardhouse where it disappeared to the left through a tunnel.

That looks likely. Now how to get there without the raiders seeing me? How about a bit of a distraction?

Toby scurried round behind the guardhouse and found a pile of mossy stones lying there. He stuffed some of them down into his pockets, and stumbled round the edge of the building. Here he had a view of the bridge and the edge of the vast dry moat. He stood up just out of sight of the raiders, and with all the strength he could muster, threw the stones as far as he could into the moat. The first one fell short of his target but the second, third and fourth flew through the air and landed in the moat. He could hear them rattling against the stone walls as they bounced and thudded down onto the grass below.

"What was that?" an angry voice boomed out.

"Must be the dogs!" another shouted. Then there was a loud CRACK! as one of them fired his gun into the darkness of the moat. Toby didn't wait. He sped round the back of the guardhouse and sprinted for all he was worth down the path towards the tunnel.

"There goes the kid!" someone bellowed behind him.

"Don't worry about him now. Keep your eyes peeled for those dogs!" Toby heard the Captain shout.

Toby reached the black inside of the tunnel and stopped to catch his breath, panting heavily. The walls bounced the gasps back to him in an eerie echo and as he tried to still his breathing, he sensed someone else was in the tunnel. But who? Was it one of the dogs? Out of the damp and darkness a small brown hand appeared and touched his arm. Toby jumped.

"What? Tash?" he hissed hoarsely. "You gave me a fright! Where have you been?"

"Watching over you," she replied as she stepped out of the shadows. She had been standing next to him all the time he had been in the tunnel. He couldn't see her eyes or mouth as she had pulled the wolf's head down low over her face.

"We must get over that bridge," she said solemnly.

"Not much chance of that now; the raiders are shooting at anything that moves. Wait, what's that noise?" Toby crept to the other end of the tunnel where the path came out onto another, smaller bridge, protected at each end by high spiked gates. The gates looked like they would keep any animal out but, as Toby watched, a pack of black dogs approached on the other side. Two of the biggest sniffed the first gate, turned, lolloped a few strides back, then took a run at it. Floating through the air together they easily cleared it, as if they were in a pairs jumping competition at a local dog show.

"NO!" exclaimed Toby, and ran back towards Tash. "We're stuck! The dogs are coming in this way... Tash?" Tash had disappeared once again.

Toby returned to the end of the tunnel, keeping in the dark, out of sight of the dogs, though he knew it wouldn't be long before they smelt him.

Maybe this muck I'm covered in will put them off the scent.

The first two jumping dogs had now been joined by two others and the four of them were prowling the bridge, caught between the two gates. They weren't trapped for long. Toby watched in horror as they took a run at the gate nearest to him. He held his breath as they cleared it and, with an extra effort, landed on top of the tunnel. They were now in the ravelin.

What do I do now? They are right on top of the tunnel – they only need to run along the wall and jump down and they'll be here!

Toby wished Tash hadn't abandoned him. She seemed to be much calmer and braver than him in a crisis. Where was she now when he needed her?

I need to get out of this alive or who else is going to rescue Sylvie and Dad? Hang on – the Captain just said they had to take me alive. I'll be better off with the raiders than being eaten by the dogs. I'll surrender.

Toby pulled a grubby grey hankie out of his pocket and, clutching it in his hand, ran down the tunnel towards the main bridge where the raiders were.

"I surrender!" he shouted at them as he ran, waving his hankie, feeling rather stupid. "Let me in!"

As he got nearer, he could see that the raiders had closed the heavy gates at the ravelin end of the bridge and were retreating.

"NO!" he shouted, as two of the men pulled up the drawbridge over the moat. The wooden section began to hinge up away from the ground, leaving a widening gap between the bridge and the edge of the moat.

Toby raced up to the first gate. He turned his head and was just able to make out four black dogs jumping easily down from the tall wall of the tunnel, as if it was no more than a few feet high. They loped towards him. They were in no hurry; they knew they had him trapped. He scrambled over the gate, tearing his boiler suit on the spikes as he panicked. He was now standing between the gate and the slippery edge of the moat.

"Let me in!" Toby screamed, feeling wobbly at being so close to the huge drop into the moat. "Please!" He heard the raiders laughing cruelly at his plight.

"HA!" yelled the Captain. "You want to be our friend now, eh?"

"Leave him there!" shouted another. "Let him stew in his own juice!"

"Aye!" yelled another. "Let's see what those dogs will do with him!"

"Please!" pleaded Toby, half an eye on the dogs trotting through the gloaming. Now he could see their long black muzzles grinning open to show fleshy pink gums and sharp white fangs. Pools of drool fell from their jaws in large splatters. He knew they'd make short work of leaping the gate.

"Please!"

The Captain motioned to the two men pulling on the chains. They stopped and let the bridge descend on its own weight. It did so slowly – so slowly that Toby didn't think it would make it in time...

"Jump!" commanded the Captain, pointing at the descending bridge. Toby glanced down into the darkness of the moat below him, and hesitated. If he missed he would fall to his death.

Jump! he told himself.

Taking a couple of steps back, he braced himself against the gate. Behind him he could hear a low growling from the four dogs. There was no time. He ran towards the bridge and pushed off with all his might when his right foot struck the slippery moat edge. He flung his arms forward while his legs flailed in mid air, cycling round and round as if he was riding an imaginary bike. Time stood still as Toby reached out to grab the edge of the bridge, which was suspended about five feet in mid air.

"YES!" he screamed. His hands found a hold on the greasy wooden edge, and he threw his elbows and upper arms onto the bridge. He was now dangling high over the moat, his legs scrabbling uselessly in mid air. He didn't dare look down but concentrated on trying to fling one leg up and over. Just then, the Captain strode forward, grasped the back of Toby's muddy boiler suit, picked him up and flung him to safety in the middle of the bridge.

"Let that be a lesson to you, kid. Don't ever run away from us, eh? You may think you're like a cat

with nine lives but you're fast running out of them!...
Yuk! What've you been rolling in, you wee toad? You
stink!" The Captain wiped his muddy hands down his
trousers and marched off. Toby lay in shock, trying to
get his breath back. That had been a near thing. Too
near for his liking. He sat up and watched the dogs
slink off into the shadows. They'd lost interest now
that their prey was out of reach.

The other men followed their leader into the fort,
one of them grabbing Toby by his collar and dragging
him back inside, too. Behind them it took three men to
close the enormous wooden door and slam the thick
metal bolts across it.

What's going to happen to me now?

Inside the fort the Captain was busy shouting orders
at the rest of the raiders. They were congregated in the
square in front of the prison. It was dark, and the men
near the Captain held lanterns. The flickering light
threw scary shadows across the grass. The raiders were
a motley bunch of various sizes and ages, dressed in
old army gear, dirty and unkempt. Toby tried not to
stare as he was pulled and pushed through the crowd.

As the wind tossed the light from the lanterns
across their scarred and battered faces, the men looked
rough. Most had lurid tattoos decorating their hands,
necks and arms, but none seemed to have the red and
black NC emblazoned on their wrists. They were all
holding some weapon or other: shot guns, rifles, even
sabres. They were anxious and jittery, shouting out
questions to the Captain, who was trying to reassure
them that the dogs couldn't get into the fort.

Some of them looked surprisingly young. One was probably about the same age as Toby, though the boy was trying to look older by posturing and showing off his gun.

Where have they all come from?

When he and his family had lived in the lighthouse at Collieston, before the dogs drove them out, they hardly saw anybody after the red fever. The only good people they had met had been the crew of a peace ship, Jamie and his mum, and Magnus, who had rescued them and let them stay on his minesweeper.

Toby was dragged across the whole fort, through the two large courtyards, past the lines of Georgian houses with their dark windows staring at him like black eyes. There were more men down in the bottom square where the barracks were resounding with shouted commands. As they ran in and out of buildings, collecting arms and throwing belts of ammo over their shoulders, Toby could see that these were different men from the others. They looked better equipped and even in the shadowy light thrown from the barracks, he could make out that they were fitter, cleaner and were wearing smart navy-blue uniforms.

Are these the chosen ones? Do they have the same tattoo as the Captain? he wondered, as he dragged his feet slowly over the pebbled courtyard, trying hard to get a better look.

"Hurry up, kid!" his captor snarled, shoving Toby with his hand.

"Yeah, yeah, I'm hurrying," replied Toby. They seemed to be headed for the far courtyard where the church stood.

For the first time that day, Toby felt his heart lift a little. If he was put in the church, he knew exactly what he was going to do.

"You're not going to lock me in the church are you?" Toby asked the man, feigning fright.

"Yeah, serve you right if the ghosties get you, you smelly brat!" the man snapped back, pushing Toby hard into the church porch and through the door, which he then locked. "And don't get any ideas about escaping or else this time I'll personally feed you to the dogs!"

Toby stood in the quietness of the church aisle and waited. It wouldn't be wise to go straight to the trapdoor in case the man came back.

After a few minutes had passed, he groped his way in the dark down the aisle of pews to the back of the church, and pulled across the curtain to reveal the vestry door.

I hope that Tash got back ok. I'm starving – wonder what she's got in her store for dinner?

He felt good and warm with the expectation of something hot to eat, in a safe place where he could relax, at least for a short while. His brain felt like it was spinning out of control. He needed some time to sort out what had happened and to formulate a plan.

If I can just lie down for a little while and have a nap, then I'll feel better. I must think about my mission. I must get going and find where Dad and Sylvie are being held. I must — What? What's wrong with this door?

Toby rammed the handle to the vestry door hard down, but it didn't budge.

"What's going on?" he cried, leaning all his weight onto the door handle.

I don't believe it. The door's locked. What was Tash thinking of? She's gone and locked me out.

8. The Invasion

Toby leant against the door and slumped to the floor, burying his head in his hands. The last two days had been so hard, leaving him feeling like a limp teddy someone had pulled all the stuffing out of. Every time he thought he was getting a step nearer his dad and Sylvie, something bad happened.

The biggest mistake I made was believing that Tash was a friend and was going to help me. Going with her has only made the situation worse with the raiders. Now they hate me and I'm still being held captive. I might as well have stayed in that prison.

Toby knew that this was harsh, after all Tash had shown him her den and fed him a good meal. But then she had run off leaving him to face the angry raiders alone.

I must trust no one from now on. I'm better off on my own.

Toby wiped his snotty nose on the cuff of his jacket and pulled himself slowly to standing. His bruises still ached. He put his hand to the back of his head to feel how the lump was faring. Dried blood clumped around the large egg-shaped bump on his skull.

Good one, that! Wait till I show it to Sylvie. She'll be dead impressed... if I ever find her.

Toby froze. He had heard a noise – a sharp intake of breath, like a... like a dog sniffing the air? He pulled back the curtain and stared down into the darkness of the church aisle, the hairs on his head prickling with apprehension. Something rustled in the blackness of the altar area at the other end of the church. It was crawling down the aisle towards him. He could hear its shallow breathing, and a scratchy scraping noise of claws on the smooth tiled floor. Whatever it was, it was getting nearer and nearer.

Toby pushed himself back as far as he could against the door and slowly stood up. Outside, someone was crossing the courtyard carrying a lantern. The light bounced up into the vaulted wooden ceiling of the church and glinted in the eye of whatever was drawing near, dancing off its sharp fangs.

Hold on a mo – those eyes aren't moving...

"Tash," he called, "is that you?"

The fanged thing slid slowly along the floor until it reached the vestry door. Then suddenly it reared up to reveal Tash hiding under her wolf coat.

"It's me," she whispered conspiratorially, as if they were being overheard.

"What are you up to?" Toby asked. "You seem to take great fun from frightening the life out of me. I'm not sure my heart can stand any more scares, thanks."

"I'm sorry your heart isn't strong, but I was thinking the men might be watching here."

"No, they're too busy trying to keep the dogs out. Anyway, where have you been? And why did you lock me out?"

"I didn't know they'd put you in here. I always keep the door locked. But you'll be happy when I tell what I've found out. Now let's go below and eat."

"Great," said Toby, "I'm starving."

On reaching the kitchen down in the cave, Tash rummaged through some cupboards and put a large bowl of cereal covered with sweet, sticky condensed milk in front of Toby.

"There's no time to cook, but here's some sugar – it's good for energy," she said, tucking into a large mouthful of muesli with dried apricots.

"Yummy," said Toby through a mouthful of the sugary goo. "Ok, so where did you go and what have you found out?"

Tash started to tell Toby about where she had been since leaving him in the tunnel on the ravelin. He interrupted as nicely as he could,

"I don't mean to sound rude, Tash, but d'you think you could take off that wolf thing? The smell's putting me off my food."

"Yeah, sure." Tash pulled off the offending article and threw it over the settee. Then she told Toby about how she had got back into the fort by climbing underneath the main bridge, clinging to the wooden joists. She had waited until the raiders were distracted by him, then had slipped over the side of the bridge and into the fort.

She's much braver than me. I bet she thinks I'm a right coward.

"So what did you find out?" he asked her.

"I hid in the stores where the men keep guns and ammo. They came in all excited. They'd heard the dog howling and then there was a big commotion. Some of them were saying they want to leave now and go to the other collecting station," she said, scraping the last of the condensed milk from her bowl.

"Did they say where that was, or say anything else about the General?" asked Toby.

"Sounds like he's a very clever man, and very powerful. He seems to have some sort of hold over them. They're all scared of him and do as he says: he says to kidnap people, and they do it. They gather their prisoners together at the collecting stations and then take them to the place they call 'New Caledonia'."

"New Caledonia?" Toby tried to put things together. The Captain had mentioned that name. It sounded quite nice, but that must be misleading. What had the Captain said? It was a new world the General had created. How had this General managed to gather so much power so quickly? And could he really be using the people he had kidnapped as slaves, as the Captain had suggested?

"This all sounds so weird," he said, scratching the back of his head, which had started to itch where the wound was beginning to heal.

"No weirder than your dogs taking over Scotland and dominating the world," Tash countered.

"Yeah," replied Toby, "well, they're not my dogs, but I get your point. Still, these days nothing seems weird. I mean, who would have thought that a single virus would wipe out most of the world's population? Since then, nothing has made any sense," he ended lamely, thinking of all the terrible things that had happened to him and his family. Tash looked at him sympathetically. He took a deep breath and changed the subject. "Did the men say where these places were?"

"They did mention a fort. Could it be another place like this? They said that there was a lot of stuff there that needed moving."

"Er, well, in Scotland there are some towns that have 'fort' as part of their name, such as Fort Augustus, Fort William and... Actually, they're the only two I can think of."

"Fort William?" said Tash. "That sounds right, a man's name. It was a man's name!"

"Fort William? You think it's Fort William? That's at the end of the Caledonian Canal. It's where Ben Nevis is. I know that 'cause my dad used to go climbing on Ben Nevis. He said he'd take me one day when I was big enough. There's a famous climbers' café there where my dad used to have his coffee and buns before setting off. He used to text me from it."

Toby was excited having heard where his dad and Sylvie might be. Suddenly it seemed possible that he could go there and find them. Then, just as suddenly, he felt deflated.

"Sounds like the raiders have got some sort of warehouse or depot there. But how can I be sure that's where Dad and Sylvie are?" he asked Tash. "All we know is that they have been taken to see the General. We don't know if he's at Fort William or at this New Caledonia – wherever that is. It could be near Fort William or somewhere else entirely!"

"We don't have much choice, do we?" observed Tash. "At least if we go to Fort William we might find out more about New Caledonia. First, though, I think we need to sleep on it," she continued, in her bossy, mothering sort of voice. "We're too tired to think straight just now."

"Yeah, you're right, but I know where I'm going as soon as I've had a sleep. Me and the *Lucky Lady* are heading for Fort William. You haven't got a map have you?" he asked, trying to hide an enormous yawn. He didn't like the idea of leaving his dad and Sylvie another night yet he knew he was too exhausted to take on the General and his henchmen.

"Get some sleep, Toby," replied Tash. "We'll talk in the morning."

He lay down on the settee, finding the Henry cushion once more to cuddle. He lay awake for a while trying to work out the best way to get out of the fort, past the dogs, and past the raiders to reach the *Lucky Lady*. Once on *Lady* he knew he would be ok.

"You'll look after me, won't you *Lady*?" he murmured, as he fell into a deep sleep.

Down in the cave it was hard to tell the time of day. When Toby awoke he snatched up his watch to see if he'd overslept, but the hands were pointing at twelve and three.

Three o'clock in the morning! Better get going. With any luck the raiders will still be distracted by the dogs or, even better, they might've secured the fort and gone to bed. Just need to get across the beach to the harbour. Surely there's nothing around there to interest the dogs?

He wondered if he could slip out without waking Tash but then thought that wasn't very fair of him. She had looked after him and proved to be a friend after all. She had even found out critical information for him. He felt a little annoyed that she, rather than he, had learned about Fort William.

"Tash," he gently shook her. "Tash, wake up. I'm leaving. I wanted to say goodbye and thank you for your help."

She sat up and rubbed her eyes. "Toby? You can't go on your own. I'd better show you the way."

"No, I'm good, honest," Toby said, reluctantly. He would have liked to have her company for a little longer; it could be a long time before he talked to anyone else. He was no good at goodbyes and all that emotional stuff. "You sure you want to stay here and wait for your mother and father?" he asked her, as he pulled on a dusty jacket that Tash had given him.

"Yes, I want to stay. My mother and father may come back anytime. This General, he isn't a big enough man to keep my father for long." Tash smiled bravely. "But I've packed some food for you, and I'll come to the shore with you and see how near the dogs are, too." She picked up two rucksacks from the kitchen table and gave one to him.

"That's very kind, thank you." Toby blushed as he threw the rucksack onto his shoulder. "Let's go then."

The two of them left in silence, climbing through the trapdoor and up the steps to the door opening onto the foremost headland. Clambering out into the freezing winter night, they turned their torches off. A full moon lit the sky and threw dancing moonbeams on the sea. Toby began to track left, skimming along the edge of the shingle nearest the wall. As he looked behind, he saw Tash was following.

He reached the harbour. But something was wrong. The large motor boat was now moored up alongside the *Lucky Lady,* blocking her escape from the harbour.

"I can't get out without moving that motor boat. And if I start it up it'll alert the raiders." Toby hissed to Tash.

Suddenly, above them, from the high wall of the fort, they heard a noise. Both turned and craned their necks to see what it was.

HOOOOOOOOOOOOOOOOOOOOOOOWL!

An unmistakeable sound spliced the icy air.

"Tash! The dogs are inside the fort!" cried Toby, straining to see whether the howling animal was a foot soldier or Cerberus himself.

"Impossible!" Tash yelled back, over the noise of the beast. The two of them stared up at the dog. It stood on the ramparts of the fort, its head thrown back, its hackles standing on end making it look bigger than ever, the stub of its tail erect.

"Cerberus!" exclaimed Toby. "I told you, nothing's impossible for him! He's inside now and he'll drive the men out, you wait and see!"

From where they were standing they could hear shouting, and then gunfire rattled off into the night air. There were several loud bangs and a cloud of smoke rose unsteadily from inside the walls.

"Tash!" yelled Toby over the noise. "You can't stay here. It's just like I said: the dogs will take over the fort and even if you do get back safely to your cave, how long can you exist there without being able to get out? It's madness, you MUST come with me! And NOW!"

"I can't go!" Tash sobbed. "Father told me to stay here! I must look after the caves and all the stuff Father saved and made, and —"

"It's just stuff, Tash. It's not worth losing your life over. You can get more stuff. Your father will understand; he would want you to survive. Now, come on!"

Tash nodded and followed him quietly as he sprinted in the dark down to the harbour's edge, trying to keep a low profile. With any luck, Toby reckoned, the raiders would be too busy fighting the dogs to notice what was going on down at the harbour. Flashing their torches cautiously onto the *Lucky Lady*, he and Tash jumped down onto her deck, and then boarded the fancy motor boat tied to her starboard side. Stepping into the cockpit, they looked around for keys or some way to move the boat.

"Perhaps we can untie it and just push it away?" thought Toby out loud. The painter of the motor boat was tied to a cleat on the deck of the *Lucky Lady*, so Toby jumped back over to *Lady* and untied it, throwing the rope over to Tash. Immediately the rising tide started to carry the motor boat away from *Lady* and towards the harbour entrance.

"Toby! Save me! I can't swim!" shouted Tash from the cockpit. Toby assessed the widening gap between the two boats and realised that the motor boat was moving too fast for him to jump across.

Oh no! Not in the water again!

He arched his back and dived into the dark swirling waters of the harbour. If he didn't reach the motor boat before it got to the harbour entrance, it would be smashed to bits, and Tash would be thrown into the icy water, *and* she couldn't swim, *and* all the raiders would descend upon them.

The cold hit his chest like a brick, and he felt the air being torn from his lungs. Choking, he took a deep breath and struck out for the boat. If he didn't get there fast the cold would suck the very life from him.

"TOBY! HERE!" Tash was leaning over the side, holding out a lifebuoy. He grabbed for it and felt her strong arms pulling it through the water and up to the boat. She grasped his jacket and hauled him over the side.

"You're safe now," she cried.

Shaking with the cold, Toby looked back to the shore. Two men were running towards the harbour with powerful searchlights, and AK47 rifles raised to their shoulders.

"Raiders! Let's get out of here!" Toby searched frantically for the keys to start the motor.

"You looking for these?" Tash held them out to him.

"Thanks!" he shouted back, pushing one into the ignition and bashing a black button on the controls. Luck was with him: immediately, the engine jumped into life, shaking the boat with its deep guttural rumble. He pushed the throttle gently forward, gripping the steering wheel, aware that this boat was completely different from *Lady*. One notch too far on the throttle would put them through the harbour wall.

Steady. Now, don't lose it – take it smoothly. This boat has a powerful engine. Like the difference between driving Dad's old Land Rover and driving a Ferrari.

As the boat swiftly accelerated, the harbour wall loomed. Toby spun the steering wheel hard to his right, swinging the prow out of danger, and throwing a massive wave up in the boat's wake. The tower of water hit the harbour wall, knocking the two raiders clean off their feet.

"YEAH! HIGH FIVE TO YOU, TOBES!" shrieked Tash, who had been thrown sideways onto the floor of the cockpit. "Amazing!"

How did I do that? No idea! Well, I'll pretend that I meant it!

Just then a bullet whistled past his left ear and ricocheted off the shiny chrome rail of the cockpit.

"GET DOWN, TASH! They're firing at us!"

"Put your foot down, Tobes!"

"Here goes!" Toby tried to half squat to make a smaller target for the raiders, and he hit the throttle hard. He felt the powerful surge of the engine as the boat leapt forward, ploughing a wide path through the mouth of the harbour and out into the sea.

The two of them stayed squatting down in the cockpit until the boat was well clear of the harbour. Toby was shaking so hard with the icy coldness of his wet clothes that his teeth were chattering. Still, he couldn't resist a look behind him at the *Lucky*

Lady. She was sitting alone, caught in the powerful searchlights that the raiders were sweeping across the dark waters. He felt a mixture of emotions: happy to have escaped and to be at last on the way to rescue his dad and Sylvie, and sad to say goodbye to his old boat.

Goodbye Lady, *I'm sorry to leave you behind but I've no choice. There's no going back now. I just hope this boat looks after us as well as you did. I wonder if I'll ever see you again?*

9. A New Boat

The raiders' searchlights splashed against the beach and the harbour walls, throwing strange patterns onto the foaming waves. Clouds scudded across the sky and revealed the full moon, bathing the scene in silvery light. Toby heard angry shouts as the raiders discovered the slashed sides on their inflatable.

Ha! They won't be chasing us in that!

"Here, I found this," Tash handed him a tartan blanket. He draped it around his shaking shoulders, rubbing his arms with one hand as he steered with the other.

"Th-thanks," he stuttered, through chattering teeth.

"Look!" she pointed to the fort, which was lit from inside with an orange glow.

"What the..." Toby eased off the throttle to slow the boat and get a better look. He felt they were reasonably safe from the clutches of the raiders now and anyway the Captain and his men had worse problems than he and Tash stealing their boat. "The place is on fire! Someone's blown up the ammo store by the looks of it."

Surely it couldn't be the dogs? Not even Cerberus is that clever?

As Toby and Tash stood on the deck and watched,

the whole of Fort George shook with an explosion ripping through its insides. An enormous ball of fire shot into the air above the high walls and burst into a series of mushroom clouds that the wind threw across the beach and over the sea. Toby and Tash gasped with shock as the vibrations of lesser detonations rumbled through the ground. Even the sea seemed to tremble.

"NO!" cried Tash. "The caves! All Father's work! All gone... buried... there'll be nothing left."

Toby took her small brown hand in his and squeezed it.

"You'd never have been able to go back anyway, Tash," he told her. "The dogs will make good use of the fort – otherwise they wouldn't have bothered taking it. I tell you, Cerberus has a plan."

"I don't like this Cerberus," Tash cried, her voice shaking. "I shall come back!" She sat down, her wolf mask slumped over her face.

Toby wanted to tell her everything was going to be all right now, but he knew from experience that in this new world, nothing was predictable.

"I'm really sorry about your cave," he said, "I understand. It was your home for a while. At least now we know where to start looking for your father and mother and my dad and Sylvie. Just think, in a couple of days we could all be reunited. Wouldn't that be great?" Toby tried to sound more positive than he felt.

"We don't know that my parents are in Fort William, and if they're at this New Caledonia, we don't know where that is. So I don't know why you're so cheerful," she replied, grumpily.

Toby turned and stared at the glowing skyline that threw Fort George into dark relief. There was shouting and screaming coming from inside the fort and Toby thought he could hear the dogs barking gruffly. Then, as the smell of burning cordite, molten metal and blackened wood drifted over them, he heard the noise of engines.

"What?" The tunnel entrance, which led to the massive wooden door where he had first been caught at the fort, suddenly filled with light and the rumbling sound of vehicles being revved up. As they watched quietly, bathed in moonlight and the fiery red of the flames, they saw a convoy of lorries, Land Rovers and battered white vans race out of the tunnel and up the track. Their headlights danced crazily over the grass as they bucketed over the rough ground in their panic to get away from Fort George.

"The dogs have driven the men from the fort!" cried Toby.

He could see the dark shadows of the big dogs loping alongside the lorries and vans, as if taunting the men.

The raiders tried to fire at the dogs through the van windows but the animals flicked in and out of the shadows, their great open jaws slavering with white saliva, looking like they were having the time of their lives. Toby almost smiled; he couldn't feel sorry for the raiders but they had underestimated the power of Cerberus. They wouldn't do that again.

"I need to get out of these wet clothes before I catch pneumonia, and I need to find a map," he said to Tash. "There must be maps somewhere on this boat. I'm going to have a look. Hold this steady for a mo'." He motioned for her to take the steering wheel, and then went to explore. He pulled up the hatch next to the driver's seat and lowered himself down steep steps to the cabin.

Wow! This is posh! And clean. You'd never think a gang of raiders had been using it.

Toby remembered his dad's efforts to get him to keep the *Lucky Lady* tidy, but there had always been so much to do: looking after Sylvie when she had been so dreadfully poorly; cleaning out her rabbit, Henry's, hutch; feeding and cleaning out the chickens…

You couldn't keep chickens in here. They'd make a right mess.

The boat had obviously belonged to someone very rich before the red fever, as everything in it was beautifully tailored to fit the small interior. It was lined with honey-coloured wood, polished to a warm gleam, and all the chrome rails and handles twinkled in the moonlight that shone through the portholes. Someone had loved this boat and looked after it.

Toby's dad had once taken him to a posh marina full of boats like this. They had been visiting Toby's Aunt Helen on the south coast of England. His dad had bored him silly taking him round docks and harbours, eyeing the beautiful motor cruisers there with envy.

I wish I'd paid more attention now. I've no idea about motor boats. Can't be much different to Lady, *surely?*

Glancing round, Toby spotted a map desk in the corner. Above it was a shelf neatly stacked with maps and books, and built into the wall was some radio equipment.

There's no radio network, so that's not much use now, but there's lots of maps. Maybe they've got the right one already out?

A map was spread across the desk, weighted down with a small hand pistol on one side and a pair of handcuffs on the other.

Toby groped around to find the switch for the small lamp; he knew that expensive power boats often had electrics that ran off a generator connected to the engines. He clicked it on and stared at the map's squiggles and lines. He found Fort George easily enough and then traced his finger up the Moray Firth until he came to Inverness. That, he knew, was the start of the Caledonian Canal that led down Loch Ness, right across Scotland to Fort William.

Fort William! Yes! It's not that far, especially in this boat. This'll go like the clappers. It's ok, Dad, I'll be there to rescue you soon. Poor Sylvie – I hope she's not too frightened...

Trying not to notice the wet puddles he had dripped onto the shiny floor of the cabin, Toby went to look for some dry clothes.

"Look at these," he shouted up the steps to Tash, having discovered a whole chest of beautiful sailing clothes: a pile of new polo shirts in green, blue and yellow; a stack of soft warm fleeces with cotton cuffs; several pairs of brightly patterned Bermuda-style shorts; and two pairs of white trousers with plaited leather belts.

"Crikes! Who wears white trousers? They'd get filthy," he yelled.

Soon he appeared beside her in a pink polo shirt under a navy fleece, and a pair of navy fleece tracky bottoms. The clothes were all man-sized and drowned Toby's slight frame. He rolled up the sleeves and trouser legs, then pulled on a smart waterproof jacket lined with pink cotton, and yanked a warm, navy bobble hat on his head.

"Look at you, Tobes," said Tash. "Ha! You do look funny! Like you've nicked your dad's wardrobe."

"You call me 'Tobes'," Toby said. "That's what my little sister, Sylvie, always calls me."

"You must miss her."

"Yeah, I really do. She can be a bit annoying at times, but she's really sweet, and she reminds me of my mum. Anyway, how about some grub?" Toby quickly changed the subject. He didn't want to have to explain his mum's horrible accident.

"Grub? What's grub?"

"Grub is food. I'm starving. There's a really swanky galley kitchen down below."

"Well, I'm happy not to drive. This is a bit bigger than our rubber dinghy! I'll go and find something to eat," said Tash, climbing down the steps.

Toby decided that he would cross the Firth and approach Inverness from the Black Isle side. From the map it looked as though the road running north from Fort George stayed close to the shoreline and he didn't want the raiders catching sight of their boat. It was not long till dawn and then the boat would be easily seen.

Better remember how sensitive the steering is. It's nothing like Lady.

The smart motor boat was built for speed and, though the living was luxurious and comfy, the cockpit was just three sides of glass and chrome, partly open to the weather. As Toby slid the throttle forward, he felt the cold wind sucking at the skin on his face, making it tingle with the salt spray. He swung the boat diagonally across the stretch of water, being careful to keep with the flow of the waves. The snow-capped mountains to the north-east of the Black Isle reminded Toby of the chocolate log his mum used to make for Christmas every year. She would let him and Sylvie stick little reindeer and a plastic Santa on it then dust it all over with icing sugar to make it look like a Christmas scene.

I don't even know when Christmas is – I might have missed it for all I know.

Toby had loved Christmas with his family in their cosy cottage in Collieston. They had so many traditions, such as carol singing round the tree on the village green, hanging up their stockings at the end of the bed, and —

Oh! For goodness sake, STOP! There's no point in going over these things. Just think about something useful like how to get into the canal once we've reached Inverness.

Toby knew that there was a big bridge to go under and then he would have to cross back over to the left-hand bank to search for the Caledonian Canal entrance. He just hoped that the raiders in their trucks and vans wouldn't take a detour north and end up going over the Kessock Bridge the same time he and Tash were sailing under it.

Tash appeared with a tray full of nibbles: packets of crisps, apples, peanut butter bars and some chocolate spread on crackers.

"Great! That looks tasty," enthused Toby, snatching up a juicy apple and taking a big bite.

"Cupboards are full of amazing stuff. Lots of tins and packets AND fresh food."

"Hmm," Toby mumbled through a mouthful of apple. "I wonder where they've got all that from. I haven't seen an apple in ages."

"It looks to me as if they've just stocked up. Everything's full. Look, even the fuel tank," Tash pointed to the fuel gauge on the control panel.

"Yeah, that was lucky for us. This is brilliant," cried Toby. "I had no supplies left on the *Lucky Lady*, and no fuel either. This will get us to Fort William much faster than *Lady* could. And by the way, she's called the *Charlotte Rose*."

"Pretty name for a pretty boat," mused Tash.

They were making good progress up the estuary heading towards Inverness, though Toby kept the speed slow so as to not use too much fuel. The boat's two powerful engines would guzzle diesel and he didn't know where they would be able to re-fuel next. It took him a few miles to get used to the boat's sensitive handling, and he was just starting to relax, when:

BANG!

"What was that?" shouted Tash from down below.

"I don't know," yelled back Toby, who had felt the steering wheel twist in his hands as something hard hit the prow of the boat. "Can you come and steer and I'll have a look?"

Tash appeared from the hatchway and took the wheel while Toby edged his way along the narrow walkway to the front of the boat. He hung onto the chrome rail round the edge of the deck, which felt slippery beneath his feet. He knelt down and looked over to see what it was they had struck.

"I can't see! I need to get a closer look," he shouted over his shoulder, peering into the inky black of the deep waters. He shuffled closer to the edge.

"BE CAREFUL!" shouted Tash from the cockpit. Just then a large wave crashed heavily against their starboard side, throwing the boat to the left, and Toby into the water.

"Arrrrrrggh!" he screamed, desperately flailing with his arms to catch hold of something as he fell, but there was nothing to save him. He landed in the fast-moving water with a heavy splash, his open mouth filling with cold salty sea. His ears filled up, too, and the strong pull of the tide picked him up and carried him away from the boat. He tried to strike out with his arms to swim but the waves battered and sucked at him, taking his breath and his strength away. He kicked with his legs but it was hopeless; he was being swept at great speed towards the centre of the estuary. As his head bobbed up and he gasped for air, the boat's headlights threw shadows onto something large and solid ahead. He was being carried towards a giant concrete pillar that supported the huge metal towers of the Kessock Bridge.

Keep your mouth closed. Keep kicking out towards the shore. Must keep trying... Mustn't let Dad and Sylvie down... must...

The force of the tide was spinning him round and round, till he felt dizzy and was gagging with swallowing so much water. Even if he didn't get smashed into the bridge, he couldn't last much longer in the freezing waves that lashed over his head and into his eyes, nose and throat. Toby felt his life slipping away as the cold numbed his brain and body.

Sorry Dad... I'm so sorry to let you down again...

10. Locks and Lochs

Toby felt something push hard at his back. Had he struck the concrete pillar already? Whatever it was bashed at him again, but it didn't feel like concrete. It reminded him of his dog, Monty, who used to push at him with his nose to get him out of bed in the morning. There it was again, only this time there were two nudges, one at his back and one at his side. Nudge, nudge, nudge, now another had started. He could feel himself being propelled through the dark water by something hard yet gentle, like the nose of a dog but bigger and...

Dolphins! It was dolphins! He caught a glimpse of a silver-blue streamlined body streaking powerfully beside him. Then there was another and another. Three dolphins were pushing him carefully out of the tidal flow and towards the far bank under the bridge. He struck forwards with his arms to swim as the current slowed and he regained the use of his limbs.

The three sleek creatures swam alongside him, guiding him as they plunged through the frothy white water, their beaks half open and a set of sharp teeth ridging their gums.

"Click! Click! Click! Click! Click!" they shouted at each other. The curious noises seemed to be their way of communication. They tossed their shiny domed heads out of the foam and appeared to be winking at Toby with their dark eyes. A strange feeling of calm and comfort came over him as suddenly, in this maelstrom of water and the fury of the waves, he felt safe, guarded by the beautiful creatures.

He reached the shallow waters of the mud flats to the left of the bridge and dangled his toes down to find a grip on the cloudy bottom. The dolphins broke away to his right and took off at speed, his last view of them being their sinewy bodies arching out of the water, breaking the surface with a white foamy splash.

Toby dragged himself onto the muddy beach littered with old oil cans, plastic bottles and carrier bags. He was exhausted. The pummelling of the sea on his weary body, and the shock of the icy cold water when he had hardly warmed from his last soaking, had taken their toll. He just wanted to curl up somewhere warm and sleep.

Come on! Pull yourself together. Just one more effort. Look for the boat.

He scanned the wide waters of the estuary under the bridge and spied the *Charlotte Rose*. She was bobbing in the slack water just beyond where he was half lying, half standing, dripping with freezing water and half drowned in putrid mud. Then he saw Tash waving to him.

"Tobes! I can see you! Don't worry! I'll save you!" she shouted, swinging the boat round. Toby pointed to a small harbour where a boat yard had once been. Tash steered the boat clumsily through the entrance and bumped it up against the quayside. Toby winced as the glass-fibre hull grated along the stone walls.

"Don't criticise, she's doing her best," he murmured under his breath as he tried to stand in the murky mess.

He managed to pull himself onto the parapet of the harbour wall and staggered along to the side of the *Charlotte Rose*. Using his last ounce of energy he lowered himself down a metal ladder in the harbour wall and jumped the last three feet onto the deck of the boat, stumbling as he fell at Tash's feet.

"You're some hero, Tobes!" she gushed, trying to pick him up from the floor. "You need to rest now. Don't worry – I'll keep watch." She bundled him down the steps and into the cabin.

"Amazing..." mumbled Toby, "Did you see those dolphins? It was magic – like they knew exactly how to save me. Did you see them, Tash? I was a goner... I couldn't have survived that tide... and then they came... Did you see them, Tash?" He babbled incoherently for a few minutes and then realised he was on his own in the cabin. He peeled off yet another pile of soggy cold clothes and, wrapping himself in a thick towel, collapsed on a sofa bed in the corner. "Amazing, absolutely amazing..." he mumbled as exhaustion overtook him and he fell into a restless sleep.

"Cerberus? What are you doing here?" Toby asked the big black dog standing next to the bed, but then it turned white and Toby realised it was Jamie's dog, Belle. But then it turned into a silvery dolphin that clicked at him as if he understood what it was saying.

But then a black dog chased it away, and another big black dog with a stump for a tail was standing over him, drooling and slavering and saying:

"I got rid of the raiders and now I'm going to get rid of you!"

When Toby next woke, the winter sun was streaming in through the portholes. He could smell something that made him think for a moment he was back in the cottage at Collieston, snuggled down in his duvet with Monty sleeping at his feet.

"Do you like fresh bread?" called Tash from the galley. "I found some dry yeast and flour, and made a crusty loaf."

"Cool! You're good at this cooking stuff, aren't you?" enthused Toby, pulling on some more of his newly acquired wardrobe. This time he had a pale-blue polo shirt with matching fleece and navy joggers, and even found matching socks.

Sylvie's going to be really impressed with my new image – she won't recognise me.

After they had sat and eaten warm bread and peanut butter for breakfast, Toby felt much better. He was desperate to get to Fort William.

"Where do you think this New Caledonia could be?" he asked Tash. "It has to be in Scotland – obviously."

"Why?" asked Tash, quietly. Toby thought she was the one looking ill this morning. Her face was pale and puffy and she seemed subdued.

"Caledonia is just an old-fashioned name for Scotland, sort of... But Scotland covers a huge area.

There are massive tracts of just wilderness and mountains – we'll never find it without help or a clue." Immediately, he regretted saying this. Tash needed cheering up, not being told the horrible hard facts of the mission. "Still, I expect we'll find out something once we get to Fort William. With any luck the General will be there with both our families!"

"Uh-huh," mumbled Tash.

Toby checked the prow of the *Charlotte Rose*. Whatever they'd hit in the dark had left a dent, but no worse damage. He backed the motor boat out of the small harbour and cruised slowly round the edge of a derelict industrial estate. It was full of tumbled-down buildings with broken windows, litter heaped in huge piles, and abandoned smashed cars. Then he spotted two small buildings shaped like lighthouses marking the mouth of the canal. He swung the boat into the smooth flat surface of the man-made waterway.

Phew! It should be a lot easier from here. No waves or high seas to battle and hopefully no raiders. It should be plain sailing all the way to Fort William.

The *Charlotte Rose* slid serenely along the canal, past an old coastguard house.

"Whoa!" Toby suddenly threw the throttle backwards. The engines went into reverse, churning up the water behind them, and the boat slewed sideways coming to an abrupt halt.

"What happened?" shouted Tash from below, where she was trying on some of the smart sailing clothes.

I'm SO stupid! I should have known that there would be locks on a canal.

In front of the *Charlotte Rose* stood a pair of tall wooden gates. One had been swung back to let the water out of a deep, stone-walled pen that stood between them and the rest of the canal. Tash's head popped up from the hatch to the cabin.

"Why isn't the boat moving?"

"We're stuck. These are lock gates. We won't be able to get through the locks without help. We need to get the boat into that pen, close these gates behind us, then open the sluice gate in front of us to let the water into the pen from the canal up ahead. That will bring the water in the pen up to the same level as the onward canal. Then we can open the front gates of the pen and travel on into the canal."

"I don't understand, Tobes," said Tash solemnly.

Toby explained that the water in the canal was at a higher level than the sea they'd come from, so in order to travel along the canal they had to pass through a number of locks, a bit like a water staircase. Each time they were going up a step, they had to move the water up with them by opening and closing the lock gates. The water coming into the lock – the pen made by the gates – would lift the boat to the next step.

"Basically it means we're stuck. We'll never manage to open and close all the lock gates and manoeuvre the boat by ourselves. I don't think it's possible with just the two of us. Maybe if we were big strong raiders we could do it, but..."

Toby kicked out at the side of the boat.

"What do we need to do?" asked Tash. "Surely we just need to push the gates open and closed?"

"Yeah, but those gates weigh a ton and even using the levers to do it, we'd have to be really strong."

"You don't know until you've tried. Come on, Toby! Don't give up so easy. We don't have any choice, do we?"

She's right – of course. We haven't even tried yet. It's just... I get so tired of always battling against things. Nothing ever seems to go to plan.

"Ok, you're right. Let's have a go at least."

Toby swung the *Charlotte Rose* over to the wall and clambered up a ladder onto the lock side. He ran along to inspect the lock and the gates. It looked scary. A deep pool of dark water sat low in the bottom of the pen. The first huge door was open, and there was enough room to guide the svelte boat through the gap. He ran back to the boat and jumped down into the cockpit.

"We're going for it!" he yelled to Tash, pushing the throttle forward.

I hope this works. I'm not sure I'll be able to back the boat out if we can't close the gate.

Toby nudged the boat forward slowly, just clearing the open gate.

Gently, gently. Slowly, slowly.

He let the engines idle and steered the boat against the wall of the pen. Leaping up to the lock side, he raced back to the gate, with Tash following him. Together they started to push the huge pole that levered it closed.

"PPPPPUSH!" yelled Toby, straining hard against the lever. The cold metal was slippery and he bumped and banged his arm on it.

"I am pushing!" shouted back Tash, through gritted teeth. The pole refused to move. They tried again, digging holes into the sandy path to gain a foothold, before throwing their weight behind the lever together.

"ARRRGGGG!" Toby screamed as it seemed that every sinew in his body was about to burst with effort. He glanced to his side to see Tash's white knuckles gripping the lever. They seemed to have been pushing for ages with no result when suddenly the arm of the lever moved a little. Encouraged, they carried on with renewed vigour.

"It's moving!" cried Toby, as the towering black gate started to swish slowly through the murky brown water of the pen. They kept pushing until the gate nudged tightly up against its partner.

"YES!" they both shrieked, slapping their hands together in a high five.

"I really didn't think we would manage that," sighed Toby, rubbing his shoulder. "Gosh, you must be really strong, Tash."

"No, Toby – you're the strongman. You're a real hero!"

He smiled. He remembered Jamie saying very much the same thing to him but he never felt a hero; he never felt that brave.

"We've not finished yet," he said. "We need to open the sluice gate now. Hopefully that won't be quite so hard."

Toby led the way up to the top gates and walked across them, peering down into the water on the far side where the level was much higher. Bits of branches, carrier bags and old rusted cola cans bumped along the wooden gate. He looked down the other side where the *Charlotte Rose* was sitting in the bottom of the pen, now trapped between the two sets of gates. He knew that really he should be in the boat, stopping her from bashing about while the water gushed in. But Tash wouldn't be able to open the sluice gate or the lock gates on her own.

"Help me turn this wheel, Tash," commanded Toby. "This will open the sluice gate at the bottom of the lock gate and let enough water through to make the levels the same. Then we have to open these front lock gates." Tash nodded and gripped the large iron wheel with both hands. They both grimaced as they pulled the wheel to the right.

I hope I've told her to turn it the right way – it is clockwise, isn't it?

The wheel gave way quite easily and began to turn. Toby could hear the whoosh of water under pressure escaping through the sluice gate into the pen. The shiny hull of the *Charlotte Rose* started to dance and wobble as the water foamed in.

Oh, I can't bear to watch. I hope she doesn't get damaged or we're in deep trouble: no boat, no transport and no rescuing Dad and Sylvie.

Toby and Tash stood in silence watching the water bubbling up around the slim silvery boat. After about ten minutes the water was slapping at the same level on both sides of them – the pen was at the same water height as the canal – and it was time to open the massive lock gates in front of the boat. This was the bit Toby was really dreading.

"Ready Tobes?" Tash stood to attention at the next lever.

"Hopefully I can squeeze the boat through one side gate; if one side is closed she'll be steadier while we get on her," gasped Toby, pushing with all his might against the lever. This one was stuck, too, and they pushed and shoved and pushed again but still it refused to budge.

"PUSH!" Toby screamed and leapt at the lever, digging his heels into the slippery gravel on the track. Tash grunted next to him, pushing as hard as she could.

"It's moving!" Toby felt a flood of relief as the rusty lever squeakily shuddered away from them, and the heavy wooden gate swung slowly outwards through the water. Toby and Tash fell breathless to the ground.

"That was a near thing," gasped Tash, pushing her jet black hair out of her eyes.

"Yeah! I'll say! Come on, let's get aboard before she floats off and disappears without us," Toby cried, sprinting back to the boat. He faltered one moment at the edge of the lock wall. The *Charlotte Rose* had been swung round by the incoming force of water so she was several feet from the lock edge.

Some leap that. Still…

Before he could think too much about it, Toby had flung himself out towards the deck of the boat.

THUD!

He landed heavily in the cockpit.

Safe – but sore.

He rubbed his bruised shin. All he had to do now was get Tash on board and steer out into the open canal. Suddenly Tash landed with a surprising lightness next to him.

"Hi!" she cried. "What you waiting for?"

Toby smiled.

"Yep, what am I waiting for? Fort William here we come!"

11. Sitting Ducks

As the *Charlotte Rose* powered down the canal, Toby tried to work out how long it would take them to reach Fort William. He had spent some time poring over the map, and it didn't look that far. He glanced at the walnut fascia inlaid with shiny chrome dials.

Looks like we're travelling at about ten knots, so we should reach Fort Augustus in roughly three hours. It'll depend on how many other locks there are to get through. And Fort Augustus is about halfway from here to Fort William. With any luck we should be there just before it gets dark.

Tash was down below, cooking up something or other from the packets and tins filling the cupboards.

Funny, but some of that stuff doesn't look that old – certainly not three years old.

When Toby and his dad and Sylvie had lived in the lighthouse at Collieston, before the dogs had made it too dangerous to travel across land, they had taken the old battered Land Rover and searched for food. He remembered how excited they had been about a trip to the Tesco supermarket at Ellon, but when they had got there the shelves were empty. Someone had already taken all the tins and bottled foods. All that was left were boxes and boxes of stale crackers and plain biscuits. They took them home and ate them with the vegetables they grew in the compound and the eggs from their chickens. Once his dad had suggested killing a chicken to eat at Christmas, but Sylvie had got so upset at the thought of eating Matilda they ended up having nut loaf instead. Toby hadn't minded; he didn't like to see Sylvie cry.

"Tash? Can you come up here and steer while I check the map?" Toby shouted down the hatch. Tash arrived beside him and took over the controls. "If I'm not mistaken we must be nearly at the end of the man-made canal and about to enter into Loch Ness itself."

Toby lowered himself down the steps and into the cabin. He stared at the map. There was a bit he didn't understand. A faint blue line cut across the loch just after the canal opened up.

I wish you were here Dad – I could do with your help right now.

"TOBES!"

"What?" Toby dashed back up to the cockpit. Tash looked at him in terror.

"Look!" she screamed. "Which way should we go?"

The boat had sailed out of the canal and was now powering across an open basin of water as it entered Loch Ness. The *Charlotte Rose* was speedily approaching a thin sliver of land in the middle of the basin. The narrow island was covered in birch trees and straggly bushes, and split the loch into two. To the left the water was picking up speed as the level of the river fell steeply, causing the fast flow to tug the boat sideways. Toby hit the throttle to pull the boat out of the grip of the current and spun the steering wheel to the right. The boat swerved past the island on its left. At the end of the spit of land, Toby saw a large, yellow, triangular sign:

DANGER! WEIR! – KEEP TO THE RIGHT!

"Tash! The sign! You didn't say you couldn't read English well!" He turned to catch sight of the foaming waters beyond the spit cascading over a weir. "We'd have been wrecked if we'd hit that!" Toby's heart was thumping furiously in his chest.

It's like I'm responsible for everything and everybody, all the time!

"Sorry," Tash mumbled and went back down below.

Toby realised now what the blue line on the map had meant: it marked the position of the weir on the canal. He brought the boat back to a reasonable speed and tried to concentrate on keeping it straight down the middle of the loch. Loch Ness's dark peaty waters swirled around them, and he remembered the stories his dad had told about the Loch Ness monster. Nessie was supposed to live in the fathomless depths of the loch. Toby had once seen a very old photo supposedly taken of Nessie, but it just looked like three lumps protruding out of the water.

The rest of the morning passed quietly. Tash stayed out of sight in the cabin.

Bet she's sulking. Well, I haven't got time for all that sort of stuff. I've got to get us safely to Fort William.

Yet, as he stood in the cold watching the grey clouds racing across the tops of the snow-covered hills, he felt quite lonely. The mottled brown-black landscape stretched into the distance: miles and miles of rock and scrub and mountains that had sat quietly observing in silence for thousands of years. It was good to talk over plans and things with someone else. He hoped she wasn't going to be huffy all day. Just then he spotted something.

"Tash!" he shouted. "Come and look at this!" He heard her climbing up the steps.

"What now?" she asked moodily. Toby pointed to a ruined castle perched on the edge of a rocky promontory poking into the loch.

"Yes, that's Urquhart Castle," she said, matter-of-factly. "My father took my mother and me to see it the summer before the red fever came. We had a lovely day with a picnic and ice cream." Toby glanced at her still face. She didn't appear to be upset by these memories.

"Well, we haven't got time to stop for a picnic now but I wouldn't have minded an ice cream," joked Toby, trying to make her smile, but she didn't.

They passed round the end of the rocky headland, staring into the shadowy ruins of the castle. Toby tried not to think of the last time he had seen a ruined castle – at Findlater, where the dogs had been watching him out on the sea.

"Didn't they teach you to read English at school?" Toby asked, trying to make conversation.

"I didn't go to school," Tash sullenly replied.

"Lucky you," said Toby, not really meaning it. He missed going to school. He had had great fun playing football with his mates, and his teachers had been so friendly and encouraging, especially Mrs Patience, who had looked after him in primary one. "So why was that then?"

"I was bullied, so my father decided that he would teach me at home. But he can't read English very well, so he taught me to read Russian instead. I'm also fluent in three other languages," she said defiantly.

Poor Tash – how awful to be so badly bullied that your dad had to take you out of school.

"That's amazing, Tash," he said, trying to sound cheerful. "I can only speak English and even that not very well. Fancy being able to read Russian."

"Yes, ok," Tash turned and smiled at him, "but it's not very useful in Loch Ness, is it?

Toby smiled back.

It took longer than Toby had reckoned to reach Fort Augustus. The light was falling from the day as they left the open expanse of Loch Ness and cruised into the narrow basin leading to the town. Toby brought the boat to a halt before a bridge.

"Oh no! I don't believe it!" he cried, staring at a huge flight of pens and locks that sloped away from the bridge. It was like a staircase of five steps to lift boats further up the valley.

It looked a daunting task to take the *Charlotte Rose* all the way up, opening and closing each set of gates behind her and then in front of her. Tash sighed.

"This is going to take us ages, perhaps we'd better wait until morning," she moaned, clutching the side of her face. "We'll be able to see better what we're doing then, and we'll have had a night's rest."

"No, we need to keep going. I don't want to waste any more time getting there," declared Toby. "Hush, what's that noise?"

They both listened carefully. There it was: a low rumble of engines coming down the valley.

"The raiders! They're coming this way!" Toby cried. As they looked up the road to where it swung close by the loch, they could see a line of headlights twinkling through the trees in the distance. "They must be a couple of miles away, which means they'll be here in Fort Augustus in under ten minutes," Toby calculated out loud. "We'd better try and hide the boat. They'll easily recognise her. Maybe it's her they're looking for?"

I once hid the Lucky Lady *from pirates in Peterhead harbour under a tarpaulin but there's nothing like that here. But there was a small inlet on the left as we came into the basin – I'll try there. Better hurry up!*

The rumbling of the trucks and vans got steadily louder as he swung the boat around.

Is this daft, heading back towards them? I've got to take the chance. There's nowhere to hide her here.

"Where are you taking the boat? You're going towards the raiders!" Tash yelled, grabbing hard onto the rail of the cockpit as the boat swerved in an arc and headed back the way they had come.

"You'll see," cried Toby as he yanked the wheel hard right and the boat veered into the inlet. "Perfect!"

An old wooden boathouse was tucked into the small harbour in front of them. The doors of the boathouse hung open so Toby cut his speed and nudged the boat cautiously inside. He turned the engine off and jumped out to tie her up to a railing.

"We'd better hide, too, in case they find her. We don't want to be sitting ducks," Toby called to Tash.

The boathouse seemed to belong to a large tumbledown house set in its own grounds. Toby and Tash clambered up a mossy bank and edged their way around what must at one time have been the extensive gardens, now choked with weeds and long grass.

"We've got a good view of the bridge from here. We'll be able to see if they keep going or stop," Toby told Tash. "I don't think they've seen us – they would have fired at us by now. And anyway, they won't think two kids are capable of getting a boat this far, what with the locks and everything."

At that moment the ground under his feet started to tremble with vibrations from the large trucks entering the town. He threw himself down flat on the ground and then waved to Tash to do the same. She dropped to the ground like a stone and then wriggled up to be alongside him. It was now inky dark and the winter evening brought with it a cold dampness that leeched through their clothes.

"Can you see them yet?" whispered Tash.

"Yeah," Toby peered over the bank. "I can just see the headlights coming down the main street. They seem to be slowing down."

Toby and Tash lay and listened as the trucks and vans drove closer and closer. There was a screech of brakes as all the vehicles screamed to a halt on the bridge. They were so near, Toby could smell the acrid stink of burning rubber.

He froze. Had they seen him and Tash lying in the grass just yards away?

For goodness sake – don't sneeze or cough! We're right under their noses.

12. Full Speed Ahead

Toby lay cold and wet in the dank grass, and held his breath. He could hear angry gruff voices shouting orders, the sound of boots skimming on tarmac, van doors sliding open and then slamming shut, and the constant revving of engines. He knew that if the men discovered them, he and Tash were in serious trouble. The cold had now numbed his feet and legs but worse than that was the growing terror clutching at his throat and slowly choking him.

Breathe, take a breath and count... One elephant, two elephants, three...

A small brown hand grabbed hold of the cuff of his jacket and stayed there, gripping tight. He could hear Tash's shallow breathing not far from him. They seemed to be lying there for a lifetime, waiting for something awful to happen.

Then, as quickly as they had braked, the vehicles accelerated off, leaving behind them a swirl of diesel fumes and a cloud of hot smoke. Toby felt the air slowly returning to his lungs, and he stretched his sore, frozen limbs.

"Crikey! I thought we were goners for a moment there. I wonder why they stopped?" He staggered to his feet, pulling Tash up behind him. As he did so he could feel her hand shaking, then he realised that she was shaking all over. She pushed her trembling fists into her eyes to try to stop herself crying.

"It's ok, Tash," soothed Toby, "you've just had a real fright. That was a bit close for comfort. Let's get going, eh?"

Tash nodded silently. He squeezed her cold hand and together they retraced their footsteps back to the boathouse.

I'd like to know why those guys were in such a panic. What's the rush? For soldiers they're awfully jumpy. What have they got to be so worried about?

It took them hours to get the *Charlotte Rose* up through the staircase of locks. A bitter wind swept down from the mountains bringing a white drift of icy snow that covered the town in a frosty blanket. It made moving on the top of the lock gates slippery and dangerous. The levers were stuck solid with the cold so it took Toby and Tash twice the time and all of their combined strength to move them.

At one point Toby was so fed up with sliding and slipping and pushing and shoving that he wanted to give up. He was so tired he wanted to lie somewhere cosy and go to sleep, leaving the boat bobbing in the middle pen, stranded halfway up the stairs.

He leant on a lever, taking a rest to get his wind back, and watched Tash trying to turn the wheel of the sluice gate herself. She hadn't spoken once while they worked.

She's got such a lot of energy. She looks little but she's so strong.

"Hold on, I'm coming," he dragged himself once more to balance precariously on the path and help with the wheel.

Come on, shift yourself! If Tash can do this, so can you. Just two more locks to do...

Eventually the *Charlotte Rose* was sitting safely in the dark at the top of the staircase.

"I need to rest, even for just half an hour or so," he told Tash.

"Thought you said we've no time for rest. We've got to get to Fort William quick," she snapped back. She had put on her wolf coat for warmth, and looked madder than ever.

Can I trust her to sail the boat while I have a nap?

As if reading his mind, Tash said,

"Why don't you let me do the driving for a bit? I can manage for a while and I promise I'll shout for you if there's any reading to be done, ok?"

Toby nodded tiredly; he'd have to trust her.

"Ok, but you'd better turn the lights on. There's a switch to the left on the controls. And keep to the middle of the canal; there's less chance of you bumping into anything."

Toby went below and in seconds was fast asleep cuddled up on the sofa bed. He started to dream, a lovely happy-feeling one. He was playing ball in the sunshine with Jamie and Belle. The big white dog was jumping in the air and catching the ball in her mouth, then racing to them and flinging it at their feet. Sylvie was there, laughing and calling out to them, and his mum. She was standing in the door of their cottage, saying something about being careful... He couldn't quite hear her.

"What?" he called out. She had stopped smiling and was pointing frantically behind him. Her face turned black and her eyes went wide with terror.

"Mum?" Toby turned and looked. There was Cerberus, slobbering over Sylvie's fluffy brown rabbit, Henry, who sat trembling on the grass.

"AHHH —"

"TOBY! Wake up! You're having a nightmare." Tash was shaking him gently. He sat bolt upright and stared at the wolf-girl kneeling beside his bed.

"It's your turn to drive," she said, curling up in a duvet on the other bed, the wolf skin draped over her legs.

Toby pulled on a dry sailing jacket and climbed up the steps. It was still night and the snow was falling fast, white and silent.

Well, the Lucky Lady *might not have been as fast as this boat, but at least she had a nice cosy wheelhouse to keep the snow off.*

He turned the lights back on, and pressed the button to bring the anchor back up.

He worked out that they were still about twenty miles from Fort William, which should take them another couple of hours to cover.

Unless I just go for it. If I go as fast as this boat will go, we'll be there much quicker but maybe we'll have no fuel when we get there.

He glanced at the fuel dial. It was reading half full.

Yeah, there's bound to be more fuel at Fort William. Most important thing is to get there as soon as possible.

Toby steered the boat out into the main stream of the canal and opened the throttle to maximum speed. The *Charlotte Rose* took off with a mighty surge, almost unseating him. He couldn't help grinning as the boat powered through the water, throwing up a frothy foam trail behind it. He was enjoying the thrill of the speed as the wind blew the freezing air into his face. Toby only slowed down when he reached a low swing bridge at a place called Laggan.

Wouldn't get Lady *under this!*

The heavy metal bridge sat on a turn-table but there was enough space under it for a very low boat, such as the *Charlotte Rose*. Toby held his breath as he nursed the boat under the metal girders and through to the other side.

We should be in Loch Lochy now. Strange name, like calling a street "Street Streety"! How about Mount Mounty? Or Lake Lakey?

At Gairlochy, Toby woke Tash and butted the boat up against the side of the next lock. The two of them worked in silence. It was taking them longer and longer to push and shove the levers as they got more and more tired.

"I think this might be the last set of locks before Fort William," he said hopefully.

Toby decided it was too great a risk to keep the lights on, because they were approaching Banavie at the end of the canal. It was close to Fort William and if the raiders had lookouts posted they could catch sight of the boat.

The Charlotte Rose was now in a straight man-made part of the canal lined with stone walls keeping the boat on a steady path. Toby kept the engines ticking over gently, nudging the boat along through the darkness.

Tash crouched in the cockpit with Toby. She was still being very quiet, and Toby noticed that she kept rubbing her jaw with her gloved hand. Suddenly she stood up and nudged him, pointing to the sky in the distance, which was lit with an eerie fluorescent glow.

"What's that?" she asked.

"Looks huge, doesn't it? Could it be the raiders' collecting station? There can't be much else going on in Fort William these days." Toby gazed at the orangey light beaming into the black night.

He cut the engines and let the boat drift slowly along. They seemed to have arrived at Banavie. He could make out the dark silhouettes of buildings squatted along the canal. The engines burped and puttered and then there was silence.

"I think we've just run out of fuel," he said dismally. Tash flashed on her torch and swept its beam out to the front of them. In the flickering light they saw a huge staircase of locks, this time going downwards.

"Oh no! More locks!" Tash groaned.

"Well, we're not going to get through them anyway, unless we can find fuel. We could leave the boat here and walk down into Fort William. It might be safer anyway," said Toby thoughtfully. "It's not far and we can creep up on whatever that place is and take a better look."

He tried to sound a lot braver than he felt. Now they were close to Fort William and hopefully close to his dad and Sylvie, his mind was going numb under the pressure of forming a plan.

What if they are under a huge guard of raiders, how will we get them away? What if they are injured or sick? What if it's a trap and the raiders are waiting for us to turn up so they can capture us as well? And what does this General want with all of us?

Toby found a place to hide the boat in a slipway next to what looked like a deserted hotel. He didn't know whether they would need it again but just in case they came back this way, it made sense to secure it. Tash was in the cabin packing stuff into a rucksack.

"We need to be able to move fast, so don't pack too much," Toby ordered, trying to keep his voice light and not give away the anxiety he was feeling.

"Ok, Bossy Boots," she replied, pulling her wolf mask firmly down over her eyes.

They slunk across the overgrown gardens of the hotel and found their way onto the road. The snow was still falling in thick white curtains as they skidded down the icy tarmac, heading towards the orange light in the distance.

"Have you got a plan for once we reach the collecting station?" whispered Tash hoarsely, as they jogged along in the dark, their torches throwing bouncing beams off the frosty pavement.

"Nope," admitted Toby. "Have you?"

"No – no plan," she confessed. They smiled nervously at each other.

The main road took them down a hill and, following the signs to Fort William, Toby and Tash soon found themselves entering the town. The orangey light shone to the left above the streets and houses, deserted since the time of the red fever. Toby tracked to the right, looking for the town centre.

"Where are you going?" Tash trotted along by his side.

"I want to quickly find a place. There's something I need," he replied, doggedly keeping to his route. They came to an area that used to be a shopping centre. The row of tatty, low concrete buildings lay along one side of a large grassed square. The shops had long since been ransacked; the grimy windows stared out bleakly from behind mounds of rotting litter. On the right of the square was a glass-fronted building, the windows of which were covered in posters of climbers, walkers and cyclists.

"This is it!" cried Toby. "This is where my dad used to come for his coffee and cakes before setting out to climb Ben Nevis. I knew it was around here somewhere."

"Do we have time for a trip down memory lane?"

"Ok, give me a break. There's something here that I really need, at least I hope there is."

Toby pushed open the glass door and strode through mounds of drink cans, mouldy plastic bottles and empty shoe boxes to get to a row of shelves at the back of the shop. He ferreted around for several minutes.

"Hurry up, Toby," Tash urged. "We're not here for the shopping."

"Yeah, yeah, I'm coming but I have to get... Look at these." Toby held out his old tattered boots. She crinkled up her nose.

"Poo – they smell!"

"Yes, exactly," said Toby. His feet were sore and soggy; the skin had come off the soles and his toes were permanently wrinkled with damp. "My feet don't smell too good either!"

The large boots had all been taken, probably by the raiders, but luckily there was one pair left in his size: smart Gore-Tex-lined walking boots that felt waterproof and comfortable.

"Bliss," he sighed, standing in warm dry boots for the first time in ages.

"Have you finished your shopping trip now?" Tash asked impatiently. Toby gave the thumbs up and they both made for the exit.

As they left the shopping centre and headed up the hill towards the light, Toby and Tash could hear men shouting, truck engines bursting into life, and a steady hum of something electrical. As they got nearer, crouching in the long grass at the side of a snow-filled track, the noises got louder and louder. Toby could sense his body getting tauter and tighter as he wriggled through the snowy ferns to get a better view.

The track led to what must have been a small industrial estate surrounded by a tall mesh fence, and entered through an even taller metal gate with barbed wire strung on the top. Spotlights fastened to telegraph poles around the perimeter of the fence cast the orange light. The hum seemed to be coming from a bulky generator sat to one side, powering the lights.

Toby could see most of a large yard with several portacabins dumped round the edge and, in the centre, rows of large metal containers with their doors flung open. Parked next to the containers were the trucks and white vans they had seen leaving Fort George in such a hurry. He even recognised some of the scruffy men from when he had been captured. They looked sour and even angrier now than they had then, their faces contorted into black rage and defiance.

Not a happy bunch, this lot.

In comparison, there were a bunch of raiders in smart uniforms standing around the entrances to the portacabins. They were laughing and joking and looked relaxed and full of bonhomie.

Seems to be some sort of hierarchy. Some of the raiders are doing all the hard work while others look on. I bet those in the uniforms are the chosen ones with tattoos.

Toby crawled nearer the fence, aware of Tash at his heels. He could now see that the raiders were taking stuff out of the containers and loading it into the trucks and vans. Great big boxes and armloads of goods in black bin liners were being thrown with haste into the backs of the vehicles. Across the yard a man on a fork-lift truck was loading pallets of shrink-wrapped packets and bottles onto a lorry.

What are they doing? They look like they're moving out of here. But where has all that stuff come from? And where are all the people they have kidnapped?

Toby slid back to Tash and motioned for her to retreat further down the hill. He waited until they were well out of sight of the depot before saying,

"Seems like they're going somewhere. Perhaps to this place called New Caledonia, wherever that is.

The only chance we've got of finding out is to follow them, but how?"

Tash shook her head; she was clean out of plans as well. The two of them lay there with cold creeping into their bones and a sense of hopelessness washing over them.

I have no idea what to do. How could I have been so stupid to think I could rescue Dad and Sylvie from a bunch of hardened crooks like these? We don't even know if they are here, and we've got no way of getting in there without being caught ourselves. It's hopeless! Totally hopeless! I'm SO sorry, Dad – I've let you down. We've come all this way and there's nothing we can do.

13. Hot Wheels

Toby nudged Tash with his heel and started to crawl back towards the yard where the men were working under the lights. He could hear her chattering teeth as she slowly pulled herself through the grassy mush behind him. Then he became aware of another sound: a vehicle coming at speed up the track. He lifted his head tentatively above the scrubby undergrowth and saw a Range Rover, lights blazing and horn blaring, storming through the gates. Snow spat across the feet of the men as it braked hard and slewed across the busy yard. Some of the men swore at its hasty arrival.

A dark, squat raider with scars on his cheeks stepped out of the car and yelled orders at them. Toby recognised the Captain, and caught some of what he was shouting:

"Listen up men! We're leaving NOW! The General wants us back in New Caledonia immediately in case the dogs attack here, too. He's not taking any chances. Our work's more or less finished here anyway. So, get going! Let's have these trucks on the road…"

"Tash," whispered Toby, "they're leaving. What shall we do? We can't just stay here; we need to go with them. Perhaps we can try and get into the back of one of the trucks when they're not looking?"

"We can try," rasped Tash, rubbing her cold arms and legs under the wolf skin.

"Right, let's go for it!" Toby stood up but his legs were numb and he fell back to the ground.

No, don't let me down now legs. Get up and work.

He grabbed hold of a nearby gorse bush and pulled himself to standing. The men were far too busy to notice what was going on outside the compound; they were throwing kit into the cabs of the lorries and vans. The compound was chaotic with men running hither and thither and screaming at each other in panic. But as Toby watched, he noticed that the uniformed superior raiders kept out of the general chaos, calmly loading their bags into a van then jumping into the seats. Their driver turned the vehicle around and sped out of the yard leaving the manic workers behind.

"Come on Tash," cried Toby, above the fracas. "We can use this stramash in our favour." He grabbed her hand. They reached the gates and slunk through them, passing into the shadows behind one of the portacabins. Here they collapsed to the ground, out of breath.

"That was easier than I expected," whispered Toby. Tash nodded. The two of them lay slumped for a while and listened to the hurrying and scurrying of the men. One by one the big trucks revved up their engines and manoeuvred out, spitting snow and mud from under their tyres. Toby moved to peer around the side of the building. He could see only two vehicles left in the yard. One was a white van, the other a battered old Land Rover. Out of this stepped a small stocky raider looking like a lumberjack in a checked shirt, the sleeves rolled up to show his bulbous arms blue with sea serpent and mermaid tattoos. Toby stared at his wrists; there was no sign of the *NC* that the Captain had shown him.

The bitter driving wind and snow didn't seem to bother the man at all, as he turned to the driver of the van and bellowed through the drifting whiteness,

"I'd better go look for that tool box. It must be in there somewhere. It's the Captain's pride and joy is that. I'll be in right trouble if I go without it!"

"You'd better get a move on, Carl. We're supposed to be travelling in convoy for safety; I'm not hanging around. See you there!" the driver bawled out of the open window before skidding and swerving the van out through the gates. Toby watched as Carl strode back to the portacabin and disappeared inside.

"Tash! This is our chance!"

"What? Are you going to hit that man on the head? And take his car?"

"No, I don't think anyone could hit *him* hard enough to make any difference. Looks a bit of a toughie to me. There must be an easier way…"

Toby slunk round the corner of the portacabin and immediately knew what to do. There, hanging in the lock of the cabin door, was a bunch of keys. He ran forwards and smashed the door shut, turning the key in the lock, then raced to the Land Rover and jumped into the driver's seat.

"What you waiting for?" he cried to Tash, who was standing outside the cabin, her mouth agape. She took one look at Toby revving up the Land Rover, then ran round the other side and jumped into the passenger seat. As they drove jerkily away, Toby heard Carl banging on the cabin door and screaming:

"Eh? Hey! What you think you're doing? Let me out!"

Toby struggled to remember how to drive the car. It was a long time since his dad had let him drive their battered old Land Rover round the field at the back of their cottage. He knew there was a clutch he had to press down with his left foot to be able to change gear. He stretched down for it but his foot couldn't reach.

Ah, Dad used to operate the clutch for me, with his right foot! What I need is to pull the seat forward and be higher up.

"See if there's anything to sit on," he yelled at Tash, who rummaged in the back and pulled out a mouldy old blanket that smelt of wet dog. She stuffed this underneath him making him taller in the seat.

"That's a bit better," Toby cried, pulling at a lever under his seat. The seat slid forward abruptly, knocking his nose on the steering wheel and forcing his right foot harder onto the accelerator. The Land Rover jumped erratically in a kangaroo bounce. He jammed the gear stick forwards, and they took off at speed through the gates and out onto the track.

"Watch out!" yelled Tash, as the truck tipped perilously close to the edge of the hillside and the tyres bit the snow and mud on a corner. "Slow down!"

"I'm trying to!"

This isn't as simple as I thought it was! Got to steer, use the accelerator, gears, clutch AND brakes all at the same time! Sailing a boat is so much easier.

The Land Rover bounced crazily down the track back into Fort William, swerving round bends and skidding through drifts of slushy snow.

"Put your seat belt on!" warned Toby, feeling the two right wheels of the car lifting off the road as he took one corner too fast. Every time he tried to slow down, the brakes locked and threw the back end of the vehicle to the side.

Whoa! Steady, got to catch up with that white van but I don't want to go trashing this into a ditch.

"What's the plan now?" asked Tash anxiously, gripping onto the dashboard with white knuckles.

"We catch up with the convoy and pretend to be one of them so that we can follow them to this New Caledonia. I hope they're not too far ahead."

As the road came down into the town centre, Toby caught sight of red tail-lights ahead.

"Ha! Got you!" he yelled triumphantly, and drove up behind the white van. The driver must have seen the Land Rover coming in his mirror because he flashed his hazard warning lights twice, which Toby took to be some sort of signal. He flashed his headlights twice back; he didn't want to arouse any suspicions.

"We can relax now," Toby told Tash. "We've got to follow this van, that's all."

"This isn't very relaxing, Toby," cried Tash. "Now we're in the raiders' convoy. If they discover us, we'll be in big trouble. And I'm not so sure about your driving either!"

"Really? I thought I was doing pretty well. Bit different to my computer games! It's better than lying in the snow, not knowing what to do, eh?" Toby grinned. He was beginning to enjoy driving. It was all coming back to him. As the van in front slowed and manoeuvred round roundabouts and over bridges, he managed to change gear smoothly and stay behind it. The road was wide and not too bendy, so he had time to eat the handfuls of food that Tash pushed at him.

"Yum, what's that?" he asked, sucking a sticky bar with dried fruit and nuts in.

"I found them on the boat. Must have been cereal bars once – they're a bit soggy now," she said, turning up the heater to dry their sodden clothes.

It began to get hot and muggy in the cab of the Land Rover. When Toby glanced to the side he saw that Tash had fallen asleep, her wolf mask skewed sideways over her face. He struggled to keep his eyes open, too. The dunk, dunk, dunk of the wipers clearing the snow and slush from the windscreen lulled him to sleep.

Stay awake! I've got to stay awake – if I crash now they'll get us for sure.

He tried to think of what he was going to do when the convoy reached its destination.

New Caledonia? What could that be? Like a new Scotland run by the General?

Toby rubbed his steamed-up side window and peered out. He hoped he wouldn't see the lithe dark bodies of dogs running in the shadows.

Through the clumps of silver birch trees at the side of the road, he caught glimpses of a large body of dark water, and he tried to work out where they were going from his memory of the map he had studied on the boat.

That could be Loch Linnhe. Wish I'd brought that map now. That was silly of me. Watch the road!

Toby's heart jumped as the van ahead suddenly braked when the road swung through a series of sharp bends and then started to climb. He had to concentrate hard; shouting and sweating as he crunched the gears up and down, sometimes having to stand up to press the clutch down fully and force the gear stick up.

Toby decided to sing to keep awake. He tried to remember the words to songs his mum used to sing with him, but "Five Fat Sausages" was the only one that came into his head.

"Five fat sausages sizzling in the pan," he sang loudly, trying to compete with the noisy, shaking Land Rover. Tash slept on.

As they drove, Toby became aware of towering mountains either side of the road.

I think this might be Glencoe.

Toby's mind searched for the memory of a history lesson with Mrs MacClusky, when she had talked about the warriors of the Scottish clans fighting each other way back in the seventeen hundreds.

Outside, Toby could make out rocky outcrops smattered with ice and snow hanging out over the road's edge, and swathes of black heather, dead in the winter's frost, crusted with white. It looked very inhospitable.

Please don't let us break down here. This is the last place I'd want to be stuck on a snowy night. Don't suppose the dogs will make it up here.

Toby tried not to think of what would happen if the men came back and found he and Tash driving at the back of the convoy instead of their mate Carl. And what if Carl had managed to contact the raiders on some sort of radio? As if on cue, a loud crackling burst out of a black box sitting on the dashboard.

"Come in Carl! Carl? How's it going at the back there?" asked a gruff voice.

Oh no! What shall I do? If I don't reply they'll know something is wrong. But if I do reply they'll know it's not Carl.

"Carl? You asleep or something?" There was a loud guffaw from the end of the line. "Carl? You still with us?" The voice was starting to sound agitated.

They're getting suspicious. Better answer it. And better make a good job of sounding like Carl or else they'll come after us.

Toby picked up the mouthpiece with his left hand. It was similar to the radio on the *Lucky Lady*. His stomach tightened into a hard ball as he flipped the reply button to ON and spoke, lowering his voice into a gruff mumble.

"Hi! Course I'm here – where d'you think I was?" He flipped the button back to OFF.

"Ok, keep your hair on, you old wifey! See you at —" but then there was another loud crackling and the line went dead.

Toby sighed with relief. The reception seemed to have died completely now, so maybe the other raiders wouldn't expect any more calls from Carl.

Phew.

The road now seemed to be descending slowly into a wide flat-bottomed valley. Toby could see only snowy grass on either side of the road as the dark mountains receded into the night. He rubbed his tired gritty eyes and tried to remember another song, but his brain had gone numb. His head was growing heavy and his eyelids felt like they had weights tied to them. He struggled to keep them open, but the warm fuggy air in the cab filled his senses with mugginess. Toby drifted off to sleep.

14. Bumps in the Night

CRUNCH!

Toby woke with a heart-wrenching start as the Land Rover left the road, smashed into a snow post and crashed to the bottom of a ditch.

BHISH!

The air bag exploded in his face.

He screamed, fighting off the white balloon-like inflatable. He looked at Tash, who was slumped with her wolf-mask face down in her air bag. He reached over and pulled it off her, throwing the white powdery nylon bags to the floor.

Oh! I've killed her! What have I done?

"Tash!" Toby cried, "Tash! Speak to me! Are you all right?"

From within the wolf mask a strange groan came that grew into a growl.

"GRRRrrr... What's happened? My head's throbbing."

"You're alive!" yelled Toby with relief. "I thought that I had... well, I thought that you were..."

"I'm not dead, you banana. But I am bashed! What have you done?" Tash pulled the mask slowly off her face to reveal a bloody nose and lip.

"I'm so sorry; I must have fallen asleep at the

wheel. I was so tired I couldn't keep awake and I tried singing songs and then I couldn't remember any more, and then..." Toby babbled on.

"Shut up," whispered Tash. "My head hurts."

"Sorry, I'm so sorry," Toby sobbed. "We've crashed into a ditch. I'll take a look."

He got out of the Land Rover unsteadily and walked to the front. The headlights were still on but shone at a crazy angle because the truck sat half in and half out of a deep ditch at the side of the road. There was steam pouring out from under the crumpled bonnet and a pink liquid was dripping onto the white snow.

"Looks like the radiator's a goner," Toby said aloud to himself, putting his hand to his forehead where a large egg of a bump was appearing. "Oh no! What if the van driver saw the crash and is coming back?"

He wiped away the snowflakes that were drifting across his face, sticking to his eyebrows and tickling his nose. Staring across the landscape he searched for the red rear lights of the van, but as far as he could see there was only blackness filled with sheets of snow falling and falling.

Toby dragged himself round to the passenger door. His legs felt funny, as if they weren't listening to the commands his brain was sending them.

"Tash, let's have a look at those cuts," he opened the door. "There's probably a first aid kit somewhere in here." He reached into the glove compartment.

"Stop fussing; I've got my own kit," snapped Tash as she pulled a small glass pot out of her rucksack.

She opened it and smeared some pink paste onto her nose and lips. "It'll be ok now," she told him.

"Fine, as long as you're ok," said Toby staring at the pink goo. "We'd better get moving. The van driver might come back to look for Carl. We'd better not be here if he does. Trouble is, I'm not sure where we should head to... I think we might have just left Glencoe but I can't remember from the map what's next. I wish I'd brought that flipping map!"

"You mean this flipping map?" asked Tash, pulling it from her rucksack.

"You're a hero, Tash! I'm so glad you're here! I don't know what..."

"Yes, yes, you're sorry now for the hard time you gave me when I was packing my rucksack, eh?"

Toby nodded. He leant over and turned off the headlights and the ignition, and spread the map over the dashboard.

"Here," he pointed. "I think we might be somewhere about here. We went through the village of Glencoe and the pass and then the road was flattening out so maybe we're near this place called Kingshouse, though I'm not sure what that is exactly."

"Where are the raiders going, you think?" Tash asked, poring over the whole map.

"Well, this road we're on goes down to Crianlarich and then splits. One way goes west towards... well, the biggest place is Glasgow. If they go east they'll come to Perth. But how can we know?"

"Do you need specs to read?" cried Tash.

"What do you mean? That looks like Glasgow to me, and east is — Oh no!... where's my torch?"

The light in the cab had grown weaker and died, leaving them sitting in the dark and cold. They both rummaged around, found their torches and wound them up. Toby shone his on the map.

"Look," said Tash, pointing with a grubby finger to a faint red circle drawn round Stirling.

"How do you know that means they're going there?" quizzed Toby, a bit put out by her find.

"Because if you look very carefully, next to it, written in pencil, are the letters NC," she said, exasperatedly.

"Ah, you're right. Look at that! I've stared at this map for ages and I never noticed that!"

I'm such a twit sometimes! Wow! New Caledonia. We know where we have to go at last. But we've got no way of getting there.

"Because of me we've no transport and no shelter either," Toby moaned, rubbing at his sore face where the air bag had hit him. "We can't trek across these mountains in this weather." He glanced at Tash. Would she be able to walk anywhere? "I think we should head towards this Kingshouse place. There may be shelter there. We can't stay here."

Tash nodded and climbed stiffly out of the truck. She looked awful. There was blood and pink gunge splodged all over her face, which was swollen and puffy.

I hope she's going to be ok.

Reluctantly Toby and Tash left the Land Rover and set off into the wintry night, clutching whatever they could carry. Toby had discovered a box of custard creams, a pile of plastic bags and some tins of cola, while Tash had stuffed her rucksack with bags of Haribo sweets she had found under the seat, and the smelly dog blanket. Most of the stuff was too heavy: boxes of spanners, wrenches, bags of nails, nuts, bolts and washers.

"Looks like Carl was planning to build something," observed Toby, poking about in the back of the Land Rover. "See all these tools, and there's even some electrical equipment: drills, a chainsaw and a wood planer. They must have electricity in this New Caledonia, though I'm surprised they didn't take that generator with them."

"Maybe they didn't have time."

"They were certainly in a hurry. The dogs seem to have upset the General – that's for sure."

The two of them huddled together for warmth as they set off across the snowy heather, branching out to the left, hoping to come across the place known as Kingshouse. Toby was thankful for the new boots: they were dry and warm and comfy. The thing he had hated most about living on the *Lucky Lady* was that everything was always clammy and cold. Even his clothes in the mornings had been heavy with the damp, and there never seemed to be time to dry anything out in front of their little stove.

I'd love to be cuddled up in front of that stove right now. Me and Sylvie and Henry would be all cosy, wrapped up together in a big blanket, toasting our toes.

Toby thought about Sylvie. Was she at this place near Stirling now? Or was she in one of the big trucks motoring through the snow to get there? He tried to concentrate on putting one tired foot in front of the other through the thick crispy heather. Tash plodded on silently beside him, the wolf skin tied tightly round her.

She's brave – a lot of girls I knew wouldn't have managed to get this far, even without me almost killing them in a car crash. Mind you, a lot of the boys wouldn't have been so uncomplaining either.

He remembered some of the girls he used to play with in the village as being very sporty and playing football with the boys on the green near the playground, so maybe it was unfair of him to think girls were softies.

Toby was so tired he began to meander in his tracks, wobbling this way and that. But just as he thought he couldn't go further, he heard Tash cry out:

"See! Something ahead…" The wind snatched at her words.

Toby lifted his head and saw a cluster of buildings huddled to the right of the track. If Tash hadn't spotted them in the dark he would have walked straight by them.

"Well done, you." He hardly had the strength to speak.

They trudged into a muddy yard and saw a sign hanging down in front of a neglected-looking building:

THE KINGSHOUSE HOTEL

"Great!" cried Toby, "I wonder if they have room service?" He fought his way through the drifts of snow up to the front door and pushed it open. It swung creakily on its hinges to reveal a glass porch, the door of which was locked. Tash staggered in beside him. Toby took one look at her drooping shoulders and half-closed eyes and sprang into action.

"Move," he ordered. "We need to get inside quick." He picked up a stone from the yard and smashed a pane of glass then put his hand through the jagged hole and unlocked the door from the inside. It opened and Tash fell into the hallway, to land on a thick red carpet.

"Mmm... Smells so nice and clean. Can we stay here forever?"

"We've got to get you warmed up."

"It's comfy here," she mumbled drowsily.

Toby was so glad to have stopped walking in the snow and cold. He, too, wanted to drop asleep, snuggling into the comfy carpet. He would sleep and sleep until the spring came with its warm days again and then he would wake up to sunshine.

But he knew he couldn't do that. He had to get Tash warmed up fast. If she went to sleep now she might not wake up again.

15. Hairy Highlands

"Tash! Get up! You're not sleeping here," shouted Toby. Tash raised her head slightly from the depths of the plush carpet and stared at him with vacant eyes.

"I'm ok." She grinned and then giggled. This really worried Toby. She was acting like he had felt once after drinking some of his dad's homemade beer: stupidly light-headed, as if he was floating, disconnected from the earth. His dad had given him a terrible row but Toby pointed out it hadn't been entirely his fault – the beer had been in an Irn Bru bottle.

Toby dragged Tash by her arms through the hotel lobby. She was laughing and singing: "The wheels on the bus go round and round, round and round, round and round…"

"Hush, Tash, at least sing something decent," Toby begged her, as he struggled to pull her through the doorway. He managed to get her as far as a large sitting room where he plonked her on a settee. He found a pile of tartan woollen blankets stacked on a chair and threw them over her, pulling off her wet boots and tucking her feet into the warm folds.

"Must get her warm," he mumbled, stumbling round the empty rooms, searching for something to make some heat. He swung open a heavy oak door and found himself in a large dusty dining room with a thick red carpet, and windows draped in plush velvet curtains. A dozen tables and chairs were set out as if waiting for the diners to arrive. A thick layer of dust dulled the fine crystal glasses and ornate silver cutlery.

Toby grabbed one of the fancily carved wooden chairs and threw it across the room. Its delicate spindly legs crashed to the floor and broke into several pieces. He snatched them up.

Sorry chair – I don't like to do this but I need some firewood! Now to find kindling and some way to light a fire.

Clutching the remains of the chair, Toby staggered back into the sitting room. The singing had stopped. Tash was fast asleep.

"NO! Wake up, Tash!" Toby cried, shaking her limp arms frantically. "You've got to wake up – you've got hypothermia. You could die!"

Tash mumbled something unintelligible under her breath but didn't open her eyes.

Toby stacked the chair in the grate of the large Victorian fireplace and glanced around. There was a dusty lighter sitting on top of the mantelpiece and some old faded newspapers in a log basket next to the hearth. He crunched up the paper into balls and stuffed them into the grate, then, shaking the lighter, he flicked the flint with his thumb. There was no spark.

Come on – light! Please!

Time and again he rolled his thumb over the ridged wheel until his skin was sore. Just as he was about to give up and search again, a tiny flicker spat from the lighter.

Great! Just in time!

Kneeling down, he held it carefully to the pile in the grate and, as the paper singed black and started to catch light, he leant and blew gently. The flames fanned through the balls of paper, throwing white whorls of smoke up the chimney. Toby sat back on his heels and watched the broken splinters of chair start to glow.

Phew! Better go and get some more chairs to burn – this one won't last long.

First he checked Tash: the colour was slowly returning to her pale face – in fact one side seemed to be developing a dark red rash. Toby frowned. He had no idea what that could be.

Maybe she's allergic to that ghastly gunge she put on her face?

He squeezed her hand. It felt warm and looked pink and healthy. She was breathing rhythmically now, the blankets rising and falling with her soft snores. He checked her feet under the covers. They, too, were dry and cosy.

She looks ok now – maybe I overreacted. I'll stack the fire, then look for something to eat. Maybe there are some dry rations still here?

Toby went back to the luxurious dining room and set about smashing up more chairs. In a funny sort of way he quite enjoyed wrecking and breaking the wooden frames into shards of firewood. It eased the tension of the past few days.

He carried armfuls of wood back to the sitting room, filling the log basket. Sitting down to admire his handiwork, leaden tiredness weighed down his legs, his eyelids fluttered and he felt himself drifting off.

Sunlight was pouring in the dusty windows of the sitting room when Toby woke up. For the first time in ages he was too hot and threw back the thick rug that had been thrown over him.

Oh, that's so lovely, waking up all cosy and hot.

In the grate the roaring fire leapt and crackled, sending waves of real heat over him. He stretched and yawned. The other settee was empty. Tash must have got up, put more wood on the fire and tucked him under the rug.

Why can't life always be like this – why does it have to be such a struggle? If only I could be this warm and cosy all the time.

But he knew that it couldn't last; sooner or later he'd have to get up and start the battle for survival all over again.

I must get going – I need to find Dad and Sylvie, but at least we know where we are heading now, even if it is a long way to go. If only it wasn't winter it would be so much easier.

It didn't look much like winter with the sun streaming in, sunbeams catching motes of dust swirling through the air.

"You awake?" called a voice from somewhere.

"Yeah, and I'm waiting for my breakfast," Toby called back.

"Very funny! You missed breakfast – it's now lunch, and it's about to be served in the lounge."

"In the lounge? How posh! Ok, coming." Toby pulled himself to standing, noticing how weak his legs were. Sitting by the fire was a large pair of towelling slippers embroidered with "The Kingshouse Hotel". He slipped them on and sighed. There was nothing as good as warm feet after a cold walk in the snow.

He shuffled down the hallway and into a large lounge that had a bar curving round the right-hand side. A set of French windows on the left-hand side looked out onto a world of snow-capped mountains twinkling in the sharpness of the sun.

"Wow!" he gasped, "what an amazing view!"

"It's fab, isn't it?" said Tash, appearing behind the bar carrying bowls of steaming soup, which she set down. "Come and eat," she commanded. Toby sat up on a bar stool and tucked into his soup with noisy gulps.

"How are you feeling?" he asked anxiously, trying not to stare at Tash's red puffy face. The rash had spread to both cheeks now and looked angry and sore.

It couldn't be red fever, could it? Like a delayed, milder version than the one that killed everybody?

Toby tried to dismiss the idea from his mind. Surely she wouldn't be feeling well enough to cook lunch if she had red fever?

"Oh, not so bad," Tash replied, avoiding Toby's gaze. He could see she was trying very hard to act big and brave.

"This is a great place," he said, sucking his spoon.

"Mind your manners, Tobes – no slurping the soup, please," Tash corrected him. "Yes, it doesn't look like it's changed since before the red fever. And there's a huge store cupboard full of lots of dried food. There are tins of soup and fruit and they've not gone off because it's so cold here in winter. Same in Russia, my father says."

"Yeah? It looks like the hotel was in good condition before the red fever and no one's been here since. Is there any more of that soup left?"

"Yep, help yourself," Tash pushed a pan towards him. "And tonight we will have the best dinner ever!" she declared.

"Why's that then?"

"Because today is Christmas Day!"

"REALLY? How do you know that?" exclaimed Toby.

I'm not sure that I want to have Christmas without Sylvie and Dad. It doesn't seem right.

"I keep a diary, otherwise it's dead easy to lose track of time, don't you think? Anyway, I'm going to plunder the stores here and find the best stuff for a slap-up meal."

I suppose it wouldn't hurt to have a nice meal. I've had few enough of those in the last three years.

"Ok, sounds good to me," said Toby. "But we've got to decide what we're going to do next. We need to get to Stirling, and it's a long way to walk. We must think of some other way to get there. I wonder whether I can mend the Land Rover? I don't think I know enough about mechanics to do that..."

"I know how to get there," said Tash smugly.

"Yeah?"

"Yeah. We can ride."

"What on?"

"Ponies! Come and see!" Tash waved for Toby to follow her. When he caught up she was standing by the back door of the kitchen.

"Be quiet and don't make any sudden moves," she ordered, slipping out of the door and into the bright light of the sun bouncing off the snow.

"Hang on, Tash, let me put my boots on first..." Toby struggled to swap his slippers for his boots, then tagged along behind her through the yard and round the back of one of the outbuildings.

There, in the lee of the wall, stood four enormous ponies staring at them with large, liquid brown eyes. Their fluffy coats had a layer of ice and snow on top, and their thick matted manes and tails were full of tangles and bits of fern and heather.

"Hello," cooed Toby gently. "Sylvie would love you. She's mad about ponies." He put his hand out to them cautiously. "These are Highland ponies; I saw them once at the Highland Show in Edinburgh, only those ones looked a lot smarter. How did you know they were here?"

"Easy – I saw fresh hoof prints in the mud leading round here, and there was new poo in the yard."

It's a good job she's so observant. I never notice anything.

Tash was talking to the horses in a singsong sort of voice, in a language Toby didn't understand. The ponies seemed mesmerised by her, snuffling at her jacket and plucking carefully at her sleeve with their soft brown muzzles.

"Careful, Tash. Remember, these ponies haven't been touched in years. They're probably half wild by now."

She turned and smiled at him. "Don't worry, my father was a famous horse trainer in Poland. He used to teach the wild horses to do tricks in the circus. He even got a zebra to walk on a tightrope once. Father taught me the ways of horses. I've been riding since I was a baby."

Trust her to have a horse trainer as a dad! Don't think Mum would have approved of the circus bit though – she hated circuses. She never let me go to any.

"Please don't tell me I've got to ride these things with nothing to hang onto. I've only ever been on a rocking horse," said Toby nervously, trying to keep out of the way of the ponies' massive feet while they stomped around Tash.

"Don't worry, I found their tack, too. Follow me!"

Toby slid round the side of the barn, keeping as far away from the ponies as he could.

I don't care what Tash says, I don't trust you – you look a bit wild to me.

Tash beckoned him into a small stone building where she was shining her torch on the wall. There was a faded poster pinned up, which said:

THE KINGSHOUSE TREKKING CENTRE
BRITISH HORSE SOCIETY APPROVED
ALL AGES AND ABILITIES WELCOME

"Just as well," said Toby, pointing to the last line, "as I have no ability whatsoever."

"Ah, you'll be a great horseman when I've finished teaching you," said Tash, laughing.

Together they explored the barn. There was a wall covered with saddle brackets on which sat large comfy-looking trekking saddles. They were covered with green mildew, but Tash soon had them polished up with a rag and some saddle soap she found in a drawer. There were lines of bridles hanging on hooks, with an assortment of metal bits and leather straps fastened to them. Toby was fascinated.

"Do you really need all this stuff to go riding?" he asked, pulling a strange-looking net mask with red, floppy cotton ears out of a cupboard. "What is that?"

"It's a fly mask," said Tash, looking up from the sink where she was trying to scrape rust from a pair of stirrups. "They should have got stainless-steel stirrups – they're the best."

Thank goodness she knows what she's doing – I haven't got a clue. I'd never have tried to ride the ponies if I'd been on my own.

Toby wandered outside into the yard and stared at the cold white expanse of moor stretching away into the distance.

Are we really going to try and ride over that? We must be mad! What if the dogs are still following us? We've not got any choice though. If only I hadn't smashed the Land Rover!

Just then, something at his feet caught Toby's attention. Splattered on the white of the snow was a trail of dark red droplets. He knelt and stuck his finger into the sticky liquid. It was definitely blood, but whose was it? He followed the fresh crimson drips that led through the yard and into an old shed. Peering into the black depths he could hear the rough rasps of laboured breathing. Whatever it was sounded in a bad way. Was it human?

What if it's one of the raiders? What if it's Carl? Or worse – what if it's one of the dogs?

16. A Wounded Warrior

Toby dashed back to the tack room, grabbing a pitchfork on the way.

"Come quick, Tash! There's something or somebody in the shed at the back of the yard. I think it's injured – there's blood on the snow!"

"What!" cried Tash. "Are you going to stab it with that?" She pointed to the pitchfork.

"I'm not taking any chances – it might be one of the raiders or one of the dogs. Come on, we'd better stick together!"

The two of them edged slowly into the darkness of the shed. There seemed to be a body lying in a pile of mouldy hay at the back. Holding the pitchfork out in front of him, Toby approached it cautiously.

"It's an animal," he hissed to Tash.

"It's a wolf!" she cried. "Look at its long muzzle and thick coat."

"WHAT? A wolf?" Toby blurted out. He quickly backed away from the lifeless form stretched out in the hay.

"Shush!" Tash commanded. "You'll frighten it!"

"I'll frighten it? It's frightening me!" said Toby in a loud whisper. "I've never been this near to a wolf before."

Tash crouched down and, murmuring strangely, approached the wolf on all fours. Toby could now see that the creature had a grey grizzled head with a long white-streaked muzzle. Its dirty matted coat was a mixture of brown and black and grey, with clumps of ice and snow stuck to the longer fluffy hair on its belly.

"Must have just got here," observed Toby, still holding his pitchfork in a defensive position. "Careful, Tash! Don't get too near!"

"It's ok – I'll be fine."

"Ha! Don't tell me – your dad was once a famous wolf trainer in Poland?"

"Yes, how did you guess? Well, actually, he looked after the wolves in the Highland Wildlife Park. He worked there as a ranger. I used to go with him and help."

I might have known! But this isn't any domesticated, safari-park wolf – this is a wild one.

As if reading his mind, Tash said,

"This is a domesticated wolf. Look – he's a wolf hybrid. That's part dog and part wolf, though they look just like wolves. There used to be a craze for keeping them as pets, but most people didn't know how to train them properly. When the owners couldn't handle them anymore they turned them out on the hills to fend for themselves. My father used to find them dumped in the wildlife park." Tash offered her fist to the wolf-dog. It took one sniff and then licked her hand.

"I bet this chap was a pet once, before the red fever," she continued. "That's probably why he's come looking for humans when he's ill."

"What's wrong with him?" asked Toby.

"Not sure – he's got a wound on his foot, but one of the ponies could have stood on him when he was snooping round here. Looks more like he's just exhausted and weak from hunger. He's an old boy, so maybe he couldn't keep up with the pack and they left him behind?"

"Pack?" yelped Toby. "So you think there's more than one of them?"

"There's bound to be. Wolves don't usually live alone, and there were a lot of wolves in wildlife parks all over Scotland. They'll have got free and been breeding for the last three years. There're probably loads of them by now."

"Really? What a horrible thought. So it's not just the dogs and the raiders we have to worry about, then?"

"Here, you keep an eye on him, and I'll get some warm water to bathe that wound," said Tash, getting up from beside the prone wolf.

"Must I?" Toby eyed the wolf nervously.

As Tash disappeared, the wolf started to stir and slowly raised its head. Two brilliant blue eyes stared at Toby through the gloom of the shed.

"Errrr, it's ok, boy. Don't worry now..." he stammered, wishing Tash would return quickly. The wolf panted gently and kept staring at him.

"Here we are," called Tash cheerfully, returning with a bowl and some clean towels. "Oh, I see you two are getting to know each other."

"I wouldn't say that, exactly," muttered Toby, keeping his eye on the wolf. "I don't trust him; he looks a bit dangerous to me."

"He'll be fine. You just have to know how to handle them," chirped Tash, winding a long woollen sock around the wolf's muzzle and tying it gently shut. "Just to be on the safe side," she explained. The wolf didn't seem to mind, and stayed lying down while Tash carefully washed its bloodied paw. She patted it dry with the towel, and then coated it with the pink gunge out of the jar in her pocket. "I think he's really exhausted. Probably hasn't eaten for days."

"I hope he's not eyeing us up for his next meal!" remarked Toby. He wished Tash would hurry up so that he could get out of the shed and away from those penetrating blue eyes.

"Don't be silly. I'll open one of the tins of soup for him. Got some chicken noodle – he'll like that, and my mother always says chicken soup is good for invalids."

"Ummm, does she? I bet she wasn't thinking of wolves when she said that."

"Why don't you go and catch the ponies while I feed him?" suggested Tash. "Put them in the stables and then I'll show you how to tack up."

"When are we going to head off? We've wasted enough time already," argued Toby.

"Aren't you forgetting our Christmas dinner? And anyhow, we don't want to start across the moor as it's getting dark. Better to wait until tomorrow, and YOU need to learn to ride first!" Tash ordered.

Crikes! She can be well bossy, can't she?

Toby backed quietly out of the shed and went round to where the ponies were standing snuffling greedily at some hay Tash had put out for them.

"Hiya girls, you going to be good for Toby?" he asked, staring with dismay at their large bottoms turned to him.

How am I going to catch them? Maybe they'll follow me into the stables if I wave a bucket in front of them?

Toby went in search of a bucket. He found one in the tack room, and some musty-looking pony cubes in a metal locker. He rattled the cubes in the bucket under the noses of the ponies.

"Mush mush! Come with Toby!" he called, slowly backing towards the gateway. The ponies flung up their heads, sniffing the air. They spied the bucket, and then all of them charged towards Toby, knocking him flying into the mushy snow. The bucket tumbled through the air and landed in the yard, throwing the pony cubes onto the ground. The ponies milled round, pushing their noses hungrily into the snow.

"What's going on here then?" Tash came round the corner from the shed. "Haven't you caught them yet?"

"They tried to trample me to death," explained Toby. Was it his fault if the ponies were so unruly and wild?

"Come on girls," called Tash, grabbing the nearest pony by the forelock and dragging it towards the stables. The ponies seemed to recognise that someone with authority was now in control and obediently mooched into the stables after her.

Once each pony was in a stall, Tash set about putting the saddles and bridles on them. Toby watched with envy; she was so calm and efficient with them. They moved over when she told them to and stood quietly as she slipped the bridles over their heads and the bits into their mouths.

"I've called this brown one Daisy, the golden one is Flossie, the grey one is Molly and the white one is Lulu. They won't know their names yet, but you take Daisy, she seems the quietest."

"Take her? Take her where?" Toby anxiously asked. The ponies appeared even larger close up and he was carefully watching where they put their huge hairy feet. He didn't want to get stood on. He had seen the mess one of them had made of the poor old wolf's foot.

"Take her out into the yard and I'll show you how to get on," commanded Tash.

Toby did as he was told and tugged at Daisy's reins.

"Come on, Daisy, be good for me," he pleaded. He was not looking forward to the next half an hour or so. The ponies looked just as dangerous as the wolf.

Daisy lazily followed him over to a mounting block in the corner of the yard, and stood like a rock as he clambered clumsily into the saddle. Sitting up, Toby had the feeling of being a long way from the ground. Fumbling, he tried to get his feet into the stirrups but they turned this way and that and refused to let his toes onto them.

"Here," said Tash, grabbing hold of his lower leg. "If you keep your legs back here you'll find it a lot easier." She slipped his foot into a stirrup and then went round the other side to do the same to the other foot.

"Now all you have to do is kick and steer, ok?" commanded Tash.

Toby nodded. She made it sound so easy. But from up where he was sat it felt very strange, especially when Daisy started to move forwards, her huge frame swinging from the left to the right.

"We'll go into the front garden of the hotel. It might not be too bumpy there," said Tash, walking alongside Daisy. "When you feel her slowing down, all you need to do is give a kick with your feet, like so!" She grabbed his ankle and swung it back to give a soft thump on Daisy's side. Daisy hardly flinched and kept lumbering forwards.

"Feels like she's going too fast already!" cried Toby, clutching on to the front of the saddle.

"Get a grip! You're only walking! We'll have to travel a lot faster than this if we're to get across the moor in daylight."

Is this such a good idea? I'm not going to be able to stay on this thing at speed!

Daisy plodded on until they came to a flat piece of ground in front of the hotel that must at one time have been a large, gravelled car park. Tash positioned herself in the middle and proceeded to shout commands at Toby while he tried to ride Daisy around her.

"Keep your heels down! Sit up straight! Watch where you're going! Steer! You're going to crash into that bush if you don't look out! Pull on the reins!"

It was a lot harder than Toby thought it was going to be. There was so much to think about. Once he had mastered holding the reins properly he then had to think about kicking Daisy and steering her at the same time.

"Ok, now let's try the trot!" called Tash, who was stood clutching a woolly scarf to her swollen face. Toby kicked furiously and Daisy lurched into a trot, nearly unseating him. He grabbed hold of her tangled mane and tried to follow Tash's instructions to rise up and down in time to the swinging movement of the pony.

"Can we stop now?" he begged breathlessly. "I'm exhausted! And my bum's getting sore!"

"Ok. That'll do – but you're going to have to try harder tomorrow otherwise you'll never keep up!" She started to walk back towards the hotel, her shoulders drooping.

Never mind about me – how's she going to cope with a long journey? She doesn't look great at all. Wish she'd tell me what's wrong.

Daisy was keen to return to her friends and Toby left the reins hanging on her neck as she strode back to the yard. Slipping down from her back, he unbuckled the girth strap and pulled the saddle off.

"Are you ok?" he asked Tash while she unbridled the pony.

"I'm fine," Tash snapped back.

Ok, I was just asking! Gosh, she's a bit touchy!

"I'm going to check on Snowy," Tash said quietly, heading towards the shed.

"Ok," replied Toby. "You've named the wolf Snowy?" But Tash had slouched off and he was left with Daisy. He gave her some pony cubes and a quick pat, then put away the bridle and saddle.

He went to the shed to find Tash sitting in the hay chatting to Snowy. The wolf-dog seemed to be feeling better and was sitting up on his haunches, licking Tash's fingers.

"He looks a bit brighter," commented Toby, being careful not to get too near. The wolf's piercing eyes were trained on him from the moment he stepped into the darkness of the shed.

"He was tired out and footsore. He must have been travelling for days on his own." Tash caressed the wolf's head. "He's feeling much better now he's had a good feed and got some healing cream on his pads."

"Good," said Toby. "What are we going to do with him?"

"Do?" queried Tash. "We're going to let him go of course. Once he's had a rest and some more feed he'll be off to find the rest of the pack."

"Do we want him to do that? They might be hunting us next! If we let him go he might become dangerous when he's met up with his pals."

"Snowy won't harm us, not ever!"

"Maybe we could keep him as a pet?" asked Toby. "Look at him – he's obviously an old dog. He's covered in scars and old healed wounds. Poor boy's been in the wars. He's a right wounded warrior. We could take him with us."

"No, he'll never keep up with us on the ponies. It wouldn't be fair. He can stay here and rest until he's ready to go and find his pack."

"Ok, if you say so." Toby was defensive. "I'll go and start dinner, will I?"

"Ok," mumbled Tash, stroking the soft silky hair on

top of Snowy's head. The wolf whined and wrapped himself around her.

Toby went back to the hotel. The cold had started to creep under his layers of clothes as the sun dipped and left the early afternoon sky. As he stepped into the warmth of the kitchen, he rubbed the sore patch on his bottom. Riding ponies wasn't easy and tomorrow he would have to ride all day across the moor and mountains, and maybe the whole day after that.

17. Happy Christmas

Toby stood in the ghostly hall of the deserted hotel and listened to the wind howl as it threw itself round the old building. He shivered.

Glad we're not out in this. Tash was right: we're better to stay here tonight.

He decided to explore the grand sweeping staircase that wound its way from the hall up into the silent top floors. If nobody had been here for ages there might be something useful in one of the many bedrooms that led off the long corridors. Toby hesitated – hadn't he once seen a scary movie about a haunted hotel? He shook his head and started to climb the stairs. This was no time to start being a scaredy-cat.

It was icy cold in the un-aired rooms. Everything was just as it had been left, with plumped up pillows and smart floral eiderdowns covering the beds. Clean towels hung in regimental rows next to pristine white sinks and toilets, and soft loo paper hung from the holders. This was real luxury living. After three years of barely surviving in a post-apocalyptic world where even the bare essentials had become more and more difficult to find, this seemed like a dream. Toby lay down on a large comfy-looking bed and sighed.

Wouldn't it be great to live like this always? Maybe when I've rescued Dad and Sylvie we can come back here and stay for a while?

But Toby knew that his Dad wouldn't think it a safe-enough place to live – it was too open to attack by dogs and raiders. They had thought themselves reasonably safe on the boat, and look what had happened.

Toby lay for a while then went to search the wardrobes and chest of drawers in all the bedrooms. After a good rummage he managed to find an old deerstalker hat, thick green kilt-socks and a pair of binoculars.

Clutching his finds, he ran back down to the hotel lobby. He wandered into a games room with a pool table, darts board and even a chessboard set with dusty pieces. In the corner sat a huge TV. Toby ran his fingers through the thick dust on the TV cupboard, and then opened it to reveal a pile of old DVDs.

Hey, Transformers 2: Revenge of the Fallen *– great movie!* Shrek 10 *– a bit rubbish that one. Some of these are ancient – a Batman movie – bit scary. And look at this: the entire series of* Pirates of the Caribbean. *They were Mum's favourite, though I doubt she'd like the pirates that we've come across.*

Then he spied one at the bottom of the pile.

"YEAH! Geronimo! *The Little Mermaid!*" Toby hooted and jumped up and down.

"What have you found?" asked Tash, coming into the room.

"I've found Sylvie's favourite film: *The Little Mermaid.* I promised her I'd find it and now here it is!"

"And what are you going to play it on?"

"Ah well, that's another problem. I also promised to find something to play it on. Still, I've at least found the movie."

"Sylvie will be happy," Tash gave him a lop-sided smile.

Well, she will be if I ever get it to her...

They went through to the lounge where Tash had been busy. Entering the room was like stepping into some magical fairy cave. From the ceiling and the beams of the bar hung tinsel and streamers that shimmered in the flickering golden light thrown by dozens of candles.

"Wow! It looks amazing!" said Toby. "You've done wonders! Are you feeling ok now? Can I do anything?"

"You could go and look for some crackers," replied Tash. "And stop asking me if I'm ok every five minutes!"

Only asking! She looks a bit better though – maybe she's got some special Russian medicine in that bag of hers?

Toby went off to the storeroom to search in some of the big cupboards where Tash had found the Christmas decorations. There were heaps of stuff there: dried flower table decorations, silver platters, creamy white damask table linen, boxes full of empty salt and pepper sets, and boxes and boxes of wine glasses. Under them was a box of somewhat squashed Christmas crackers. Toby pulled it out, and then at the very back of the cupboard he found another small box. On the side it said "Polaroid Camera – Complete with Film Pack". He opened it and took out an old bulky object. It didn't look anything like the slim digital camera he had once owned.

He lifted it to his eye, took imaginary aim at a tree outside of the window and pressed a button on the top.

FLASH!

Taken by surprise, Toby dropped the camera onto the floor. He bent to pick it up but as he did so it whirled and buzzed and spat out a damp sheet of paper from the front.

"What's that?" As he stared at the paper an image began to form of the tree outside the window.

Look at that! That's fab! It's a camera with a built-in printer. That's amazing! I think I'll give it to Tash for a Christmas present.

Carrying his booty carefully, Toby went back to the lounge bar where Tash had set a table with a white tablecloth and shining silver cutlery. Toby put out the crackers and then sat down, hiding the camera under his seat. Tash came through with two plates brimming with ham, green peas and potatoes.

"All out of tins!" she proudly announced, placing the plate carefully in front of Toby. They pulled their crackers and put the green-and-red paper hats on their heads. Toby read out the rubbish jokes to Tash, who laughed loudly at them all. After that Tash produced a Christmas pudding that she had discovered wrapped in foil, and had cooked.

"Don't worry," she said, "five hours of steam will have killed all the bugs."

"Tastes delicious!" mumbled Toby through a mouthful of the rich moist pudding. "I can't remember the last time I had such a wonderful meal. Thanks to the chef." He passed Tash the box containing the camera.

"A present for me?" she asked, opening the box.

"Go on, point it at me and press that button on the top," begged Toby. Tash followed his instructions and shrieked with laughter when the photo popped out the front. It then developed in front of her eyes, showing a bleary-faced Toby in a red paper hat.

"It's you, Tobes!" she cried, waving the photograph in the air.

"Let me take one of you now," said Toby. Tash licked her fingers and smeared her black hair down and then smiled crookedly at the camera, showing her pearly white teeth.

"Great!" yelled Toby as the film came out with a smiling Tash on it.

"I haven't got you a present, but what would you have liked?" asked Tash.

"Well," Toby stretched out his legs, "apart from the obvious, such as seeing my dad and Sylvie, or a new car, I suppose a hot bath would be pretty high on my list. I think I don't smell too good."

"Me too!" Tash cried, laughing.

Afterwards, they had a brief argument about clearing up the dinner. Toby thought that they should just leave the mess, seeing that no one else was likely to come there for a very long time. Tash thought that it was only polite to leave the place as tidy as they had found it. In the end they agreed that they would leave it until the morning and then give the place a quick tidy. Toby stacked more broken chairs onto the fire in the sitting room before they went to bed.

"Gosh, I'm full," groaned Toby, crawling onto his settee and snuggling into a pile of blankets. "Good night and happy Christmas, Tash," he murmured.

Happy Christmas Dad and Sylvie, wherever you are. I don't suppose you had such a nice Christmas as me. I hope we'll be together next Christmas!

The wind was rattling against the window when Toby opened his eyes to a new day. He shivered. The fire had gone out in the night and the room felt damp and icy. He yawned, and his warm breath froze into white clouds in the air.

Better get going, I suppose. Be nice to stay here a bit longer but that won't get Dad and Sylvie rescued.

Bracing himself, he threw back the covers and pulled on his boots. Tash was asleep on the opposite settee, softly snoring under a mound of blankets. Toby stretched and stumbled to the window, then scratched at the white swirls of frost that patterned the inside of the glass. He picked up his new binoculars and stared out at the grey foggy landscape. He frowned and then looked again. There seemed to be some movement on the road leading down the valley, past the hotel. He struggled with the focus control, and then took another look.

Oh no! The raiders are back! They must be looking for Carl and the Land Rover.

"Tash! Quick! We must leave now! Get your stuff!"

Tash leapt out of her cocoon of blankets and shot out into room. Toby was taken aback by her quick response; she was obviously used to crises.

"I'll get the ponies ready. You pack some food!" She pulled on her jacket as she left.

Toby raced into the kitchen and started throwing packets and tins into a rucksack.

Remember a tin opener and something to heat food on! What about blankets and spare clothes?

He ran round like a mad thing, chucking anything he could see that might be useful into the bag.

How much can a pony carry? Can we take pots and pans? Have we got room for more tins?

He sprinted into the bar and picked up the photos they'd taken and stuffed them into the pocket of his jeans.

Map, torches, matches... What else do we need?

He picked up the two bags of food then ran outside to the barn where Tash was tacking up the ponies. His fingers trembling with shock, he tied the bags onto the front of the saddles.

"You take Daisy and Flossie. Get on one and lead the other," ordered Tash.

Toby went quietly into the stable where the two ponies were standing with their saddles and bridles on.

"Come on ladies. Now be nice to Toby. I need you to be good." He undid their lead ropes and pulled them through the barn doors and over to the mounting block where he scrambled onto Daisy's back. Fumbling frantically, he tried to get his feet into the stirrups before the pony set off.

"Hang on tight! Daisy will just follow Molly," called out Tash as she rode by on Molly, leading Lulu. She disappeared round the side of the barn, heading towards the open moorland. Daisy decided that she didn't want to be left behind and wheeled round sharply, leaving the yard at a sharp trot.

"Steady!" cried Toby, bouncing about alarmingly in the saddle, trying to remember everything Tash had taught him the day before. He hung onto the reins with one hand to steer, and grasped the pommel at the front with the other, desperately trying to stay on. Just as he thought he couldn't hold on any longer, Tash slowed down to wait for him. She reined in Molly and pulled the map out of her pocket. Toby struggled to get out his binoculars, and scanned the land to the north.

"That must have been the raiders looking for their mate Carl," he said. "Wonder what they'll think when they find he's not in the Land Rover. Maybe they'll assume he's wandered off looking for shelter. Bet they head to Kingshouse – it's the only place for miles. I should have been keeping watch. We could easily have been caught!"

Toby could have kicked himself. It didn't pay to get too comfy in this battle for survival.

18. Race Across Rannoch

Toby sat and studied the frozen white moorland in front of them. Heavy banks of freezing fog rolled along the valley bottom, making it difficult to see which way they needed to go.

Tash was peering at the map, folding it this way and that to stop it being blown away. Molly didn't seem to mind the paper cracking and snapping in her ears.

"Here," she said. "This path is called the West Highland Way. It goes to Crianlarich." She pointed to a black peaty track peeking through the snow. It came out not far from the main road and Toby searched frantically up and down, pressing his binoculars to his chapped face.

"We'd better cross the road quickly," he warned Tash. "We don't want to be spotted by any raiders driving along it." She nodded and, pointing Molly's head towards the road, nudged the pony's sides with her heels. Molly set off at a fast trot with Lulu obediently trotting behind. Daisy stuck her head down and with a flying buck took off after them, Toby clinging on desperately.

"Whoa!" he yelled in Daisy's ear, but she ignored him and kept charging after her mates. Flossie didn't want to go any faster and steadfastly jogged behind so that Toby, hanging onto her rope, was being pulled backwards.

As they skidded over the road and hit the track on the other side, Toby caught sight of something in the distance. It was the white van heading back towards them, its headlights twinkling in the mist. Toby whistled to get Tash's attention and pointed to the vehicle charging along the bottom of the valley. She nodded and urged the ponies faster. The cold icy wind whistled past Toby's face as Daisy took off with a powerful surge of her hind legs. His heart jumped into his mouth as he felt the energy pulsing through him, carrying him forward at speed over the tussocky clumps of grass and heather.

Just as well Daisy's sure-footed! I wouldn't want her to trip going at this rate.

Flossie was now galloping alongside Daisy. Clods of frosty earth and snow flew up from the feet of the ponies in front, bashing Toby sharply on the chin.

The ponies were enjoying themselves galloping as a herd across the snowy heath with the wind whipping their flying manes and their tails stretched out like banners behind them. Toby would have enjoyed it, too, if it hadn't been for the threat of the raiders. He soon worked out that the best stance was to lean forward, standing up in the stirrups and hanging on like crazy to Daisy's mane.

This is just like being a cowboy! But like the Wild West out here – what with the bad guys chasing us!

As they put distance between themselves and the road, mist enveloped the four ponies and their riders. Toby hauled on the reins, calling to Tash,

"I think we can slow down now." The wind had sucked the air from his chest and he needed to catch his breath. "They won't be able to see us; it's too misty."

Tash nodded. "You're right, and we don't want to tire out the ponies too quickly either." She brought Molly back to a walk and patted her sweaty neck. The ponies were thoroughly excited by their dash to safety. They snorted wildly and danced sideways as steam rose from their hairy coats.

"Settle down now, girl," ordered Toby as Daisy jogged and pranced behind Tash's ponies. At last she steadied to a fast walk, which Toby found surprisingly comfortable. He had a chance to look about as they crossed the moor. The ceaseless wind had blown much of the snow onto the heather in drifts, revealing the black sticky wells of the peat hags.

"This is Rannoch Moor!" Tash called back to him, throwing her arms open wide to take in the whole landscape.

Rannoch Moor, eh? What a bleak-looking place. I wouldn't want to be here on my own.

With the miserable biting wind chafing at his face, Toby felt glad of the strong warm body of Daisy carrying him along, even if she did have a mind of her own. The presence of the ponies was comforting; they were like great big bears bumbling along. He somehow felt so much safer. Even when Daisy's unshod hooves occasionally slipped on the slushy track, her surefootedness kept her from falling.

"Good girl, that's right, you follow Molly and Lulu and don't get any mad ideas about galloping off." Toby tried talking to the pony in the singsong voice he had heard Tash use, but he wasn't convinced Daisy was paying any attention to him.

As the morning's low mist lifted, he became aware of the massive craggy mountains that stood like dark sentinels guarding the moor, their snow-capped tops disappearing into the clouds. Dwarfed by the majestic landscape, he saw there was not a stick of shelter, not even a tree or large boulder under which they could escape the chill wind.

Eventually they came to a copse of tall, scrubby Scots pines and Tash stopped again to consult the map. Toby got out his binoculars and studied the barren terrain for any sign of the men. But the road was way over to the east now and Toby and Tash were headed due south.

The ponies strode on, seemingly oblivious to the cold and the gusting snow. As the day wore on, Toby found himself falling asleep, lulled by the gentle rocking motion.

He woke suddenly, when Daisy swerved dramatically to a halt.

"Huh?" he moaned. "What's happening?" His feet were numb with cold and his bottom was sore with being in the saddle for hours. "Where are we?"

"We've travelled quickly and come a good distance but the ponies need a rest now." Tash swung her leg over her saddle and dropped to the ground. "We'd better find a safe place for the night before it gets dark."

"Ok," muttered Toby, stiffly trying to get off Daisy. "Stand Daisy! Whoa! Let me get down!"

But whatever had brought Daisy to a sudden standstill was still unsettling her. The big pony veered violently around, standing on Toby's foot.

"Ah!" he yelled, pushing her off and grabbing hold of the reins. But Daisy wheeled around and around Toby, striking out with her foreleg to impatiently paw the ground. Then, snorting through her wide velvety nostrils, she flung back her head and neighed loudly straight into Toby's ear.

"Hey! Stop trying to deafen me, will you! What's the matter with this mad brute? Tash, do something quick before it crushes me!"

The other ponies, sensing Daisy's panic, started to get anxious too. Flossie charged forward, barging into the back of Daisy, and knocking Toby sideways.

Tash stepped forwards and, calling softly to the ponies, tried to calm them. But now Molly and Lulu started to stamp and whinny, tossing their heads in the air and calling out into the growing dusk.

"Get the ponies' tack off NOW!" ordered Tash, deftly undoing the girth straps on Molly's saddle and pulling it off to one side. Toby copied her, reaching under Daisy's saddle flap and fumbling with the straps. As Daisy charged to his right, Toby jerked the straps free and dumped the saddle on the ground. Now all he had to do was get to Flossie and remove their bags, but as Daisy broke free from the reins, he found himself trapped between the two ponies, their large rumps crushing him.

"Get over!" he yelled, pushing with all his strength against their wet hairy flanks. Flossie momentarily stood still while Toby yanked the bags from her back. Then he had to let go of her lead rein as she buffeted him into Daisy's hind legs. Daisy took fright, lifted a leg and kicked out, catching Toby on his knee.

"Blast! She got me!" he screamed, clutching his leg in agony. The two ponies, thoroughly upset now, snorted and took off across the moor with their tails kinked over their backs.

Tash was still trying to hang onto Molly and Lulu but they, seeing their mates disappear, wrenched the reins from Tash's hands, twirled round and galloped off. Toby watched as the plump behinds of the ponies vanished into the gloom.

"What got into them?" he asked.

"I don't know," gasped Tash, the colour draining from her flushed face. "Daisy got spooked, and she's the lead mare of the herd so the others followed her." Toby could see Tash was shocked by the ponies' behaviour.

"WHAT spooked her?"

"I don't know, but we need to get somewhere safe quickly."

"Now you're scaring me."

Toby scrambled up a nearby knoll and scanned the dusky gloaming with his binoculars. It was too dark to see much but, as the clouds trailed away from the waning moon, the silvery light picked out a shadowy building in the valley below.

"There!" he called to Tash, who was staring despondently at the discarded saddles. "There's a place in the valley below!"

He ran back down to her and hauled a saddle over each arm.

"We'd better take the tack in case the ponies come back," he said, as a sense of dread began to gnaw at his insides.

If there is something out there we'll be safest inside. It couldn't be the dogs could it? Have they caught up with us?

Toby and Tash dragged themselves down the woody hillside. Neither said a word.

The building turned out to be an old shooting lodge with a porch held up by knobbly tree trunks. Toby shoved the door open into a small hallway full of dried dead leaves. He pushed them aside with his boot, dropping the saddles down onto a wicker chair. Turning on his torch, he carefully opened the next door. The light from his torch flickered over a large vaulted room, picking out the glassy eyes of dozens of stags' heads lining the walls.

Yuk! Mum wouldn't have liked this! Sylvie would hate it, too.

He stepped into the room and shone the light on the ceiling, where hundreds of pairs of antlers caught the beam, throwing stick-like shadows onto the walls. Toby grimaced. The hall was like a cemetery for animals, with several larger stuffed heads of rhino, antelope and wildebeest hung over a huge stone fireplace.

Tash quietly entered the room behind him. He heard her sigh heavily as she threw down the bags. He turned to face her.

"Tash, it's not your fault about the ponies. You weren't to know that they'd get spooked and take off like that. You shouldn't feel bad."

Toby saw her slumped shoulders shrug in resignation. She seemed to be blaming herself for the mess they were in. They had no transport now and they were stuck in the middle of nowhere, miles from where they wanted to be.

"I don't know why the ponies got so scared," she said sadly, pulling her wolf coat out of a bag and tying it around her waist. Tugging the wolf mask down over her face, she started to take food and provisions out of the saddle-bags. Toby heard her sniff loudly and looked away; she wouldn't want him to see her cry.

He got out the portable gas stove he had found at Kingshouse and assembled it in the grate of the large fireplace. He placed a billycan on the top, turned on the gas and lit the flame. He pulled up two stout armchairs from the back of the hall, then opened a tin of tuna using his penknife to rip up the lid. Tash came and sat in the armchair opposite him, staring miserably into the fireplace.

Toby cooked up a tin of cheesy pasta and stirred in some tuna. Spooning half of it into another can, he passed it to Tash. The darkness of the surrounding hall wrapped around them as they sat and ate the dinner in silence.

"I reckon we're about forty-five miles from Stirling," said Toby, trying to sound cheery, as if forty-odd miles wasn't a long, long way by foot. Tash shrugged once more, her face obscured by the wolfish grin of the mask.

"I'd better make a fire. It's going to be cold in here tonight." Tash just nodded. Toby left the hall to search for firewood, skimming his torch over the piles of dead leaves in the porch. The wicker chair would be a start but it wouldn't last long; he needed to find some proper wood to burn.

There's nothing for it – I'll have to go outside. Don't really want to do that, those ponies were scared of something out there.

There might be a log store in the back yard. He cautiously opened the front door and peered into the blackness. Outside, the night mist swirled and burled through the dark cathedral of tall trees next to the lodge. From the depths of the wood there came noises of creatures running around: snorts and grunts and snufflings of beasts he could only imagine. Suddenly a noise he knew all too well pierced the air:

HOOOOOOOOOOOOOOOOOOOOOOOOWL!!!

The hairs on the back of Toby' neck stood to attention and every nerve in his body was taut with fear. The howl went through him like a cold thin sabre stabbing his heart. There was something primeval about that cry.

The dogs! How on earth? What are they doing this far south? ... Although that howl sounded different somehow.

19. A Bad Feeling

Toby slammed the door shut and, with shaking hands, pulled the bolts across. His heart was thumping loudly in his chest. Should he tell Tash? Maybe she hadn't heard the howl? He decided not to. She had enough to worry about.

When he went into the hall he found her fast asleep, curled up in one of the armchairs with her wolf coat pulled tightly around her. He set to demolishing his armchair. If the choice was between being warm or being comfortable in the chair, then he would choose to be warm. Beside which, he didn't think he was going to get much sleep tonight.

After smashing up the armchair with an axe he found in an empty log basket, Toby stacked up the wooden pieces in the grate and set fire to them. The flames leapt and spat but soon the warmth spread across his cheeks. There was just one last job he had to do, and that was to secure the lodge. He didn't want whatever was out there to sneak in on them in the middle of the night. He dragged benches in front of doors, propped up chairs against door handles, and pulled cupboards over cellar entrances. Then, exhausted, he slumped down in front of the crackling fire and fell fast asleep.

*

It was late morning when Toby eventually woke to the smell of something frying. Tash was up and cooking tinned frankfurters on the stove. The fire was cackling and roaring with wood from her armchair. Both of them squatted on the wooden floor of the hall to eat, curling up to be closer to the warmth of the fire.

"So," said Tash, breaking her silence. "You heard something howling and decided not to tell me?"

"You were asleep." Toby was too stiff and sore to enter into an argument this morning. "I didn't want to wake you, and it might not have been a howl anyway."

"It was. I heard it too and later there were more."

"It didn't sound like before though," said Toby thoughtfully. "Last night it sounded like a different animal, more... I don't know... more wild somehow. And it was much scarier if that's possible. Could it have been wolves?"

"Could be. Snowy must have belonged to a pack somewhere in these parts. But they were being very vocal – wolves don't usually make all that noise unless there's something really upsetting them."

"Like what?"

"I don't know – something threatening their territory? Maybe another pack of wolves?"

"Or dogs?" said Toby, his stomach lurching with fear. "I've a really bad feeling about this, Tash. I think we should get on the road now and get away from this place. I don't like this one bit."

Toby kicked the fire out of the grate, and grabbed his bag. The two of them quickly stashed their stuff into their rucksacks and set off without looking back. It was one place Toby really didn't want to see ever again. The two of them walked fast, stopping only to check the map, or to take a drink of water from a stream. The heavy pack was rubbing Toby's shoulders sore but he didn't dare moan. Tash walked stoically beside him without grumbling.

She's been very quiet – I think she's not feeling well but doesn't want to worry me. I just hope she's going to make it to Stirling.

They stopped by a derelict house of tumbled-down stones for their lunch, perching on the mossy walls to eat broken crackers and corned beef. Toby sat nervously watching the horizon.

It feels like we're being followed. But maybe I'm just imagining it? Maybe I'm going crazy? After all that's happened, who could blame me for going a bit bonkers?

Toby didn't let Tash linger long and they kept moving quickly along the narrow path that took them down through the woods. They leapt over boulders and across streams until they came to a fork in the track.

"This way is quicker," pronounced Tash, peering at the map and pointing up a hillside. "But this way is less mountainous." She motioned to the other path.

Toby studied the two routes carefully: this was important. If he chose the wrong way now, they might never reach Stirling. He looked up at the black ridge poised above them. It was a more difficult path but there was more chance of seeing something or someone sneaking up on them.

"We're going up there," he stated, starting towards the mountainous route. "We'll have to risk it."

Tash nodded and then plodded on behind him.

Maybe she's just tired and fed up? Who could blame her? We've had so many set-backs. I must try harder to be positive and lead the way.

Toby took her hand and marched forwards. They needed to cover a lot of ground that afternoon before it got dark at about three o'clock. He didn't want them to be stuck on the mountains at night.

Together they walked side-by-side, stride for stride onwards, climbing higher and higher, the wind whipping at their clothes and faces. The wide track dwindled to a stony, scree-strewn path.

Ah, that foot's sore where that flipping pony stood on it and my legs are killing me, but got to keep going. Can't be much further to the summit, then it'll be easier on the way down the other side.

Toby placed his feet carefully one in front of the other as the path twisted and turned taking them up and up towards the cloudy tops. The backs of his legs were throbbing with the effort and he gasped as the coldness ripped his breath from his chest. Stopping to wait for Tash, he scanned the hills. Shrouded in murky greyness, they looked foreboding. Then the light suddenly left the sky. A black cloud was rolling off the top of the mountain towards them.

"Snow, I think," Toby called out to the breathless Tash. But as he spoke, the rain cloud burst over their heads. The wind drove icy shafts of piercing wet needles into their exposed faces. Toby pulled his jacket collar up to his chin, yet as they climbed higher the rain penetrated every possible gap in his clothes. A freezing dampness began seeping through to his skin.

Never did see what folk liked so much about hill walking. This isn't much fun.

Toby stopped for Tash. She was getting slower and slower and further and further behind.

We're never going to get over the top before nightfall at this rate. I hope she's ok. She always seems so tough.

They made slow progress. Before long the path became slushy with snow then when they neared the summit they were trudging through thick drifts.

Darkness began to fall and a creeping panic almost overwhelmed Toby. He didn't want to be benighted on the mountain, remembering his dad's scary stories of climbers lost in snow blizzards.

He kept encouraging Tash to speed up, but could see that her strength was failing. There was no chance of them getting off the mountain before night came. He decided to find a sheltered spot and dig in.

Isn't that what mountaineers do? Dig a snow hole or something? Better find somewhere quick – she's going to collapse soon and then how will I move her?

Toby searched for a good shelter, raking his gaze round boulders and dips in the mountainside for a place where they could get out of the wind and maybe set up the little gas stove to cook hot food.

She'll feel better once she's got something hot inside her.

He wasn't really convincing himself.

"Come on," he called, trying to sound cheery. "I've found a great spot to have a rest." He didn't want to frighten her by saying that they were staying on the mountain for the night.

Toby helped Tash into a tiny cave he had found under a large boulder. If they shuffled to the back there would be just enough room for the two of them to stretch out their weary legs. Tash clambered in, pulling her bags from her shoulders, and lay lifelessly on the floor of the cave. Toby took one look at her white face peeping out from under the wolf mask and panicked: she didn't look right. He put his hand on her brow. It was burning hot.

Isn't that the sign of an infection? Sylvie was really hot when we thought she had the red fever and it turned out she had tonsillitis. Maybe Tash has got that? What shall I do? Maybe we've got some of those painkillers that take down your temperature...

Toby rummaged in Tash's rucksack, pulling out tins of food, a penknife, a small hacksaw, a battered leather-bound diary, a box of matches, a box of sticking plasters, and even a beautiful silk scarf. Right at the bottom he found a squashed, dirty, brown teddy bear, and...

Paracetamol. Great.

He took two tablets out of the foil wrapper and, filling a billycan with some snow, gave them to Tash.

"Take these and suck on this snow," he ordered, pushing them into her limp hands. He had to hold her head up while she gulped down the tablets.

As he set up the stove and boiled some more snow, Toby tried not to think of how bad this all was. He sloshed a tea bag into the water and passed it to Tash to drink. She pulled herself up and tried to slurp from the billycan. With numb frozen hands he struggled to open a tin of beans. "No toast, I'm afraid," he joked, "but some nice oatmeal biccies to go with the beans?"

Tash nodded and he pushed a biscuit into her hand. He spooned some beans into a cup for her. As they sat quietly sucking on the hot beans, Toby listened to the wailing of the wind outside the cave. Suddenly he became aware of a louder noise, one that was getting nearer.

"DOGS!" he yelled. "There's dogs outside – I can hear them barking!"

"What?" mumbled Tash, peering from under her wolf mask. Toby scrambled to the entrance of the cave and stared out into the snow-swept darkness. There it was again: a cacophony of barks and howls and whines. There must be a lot of dogs out there, and they were approaching fast.

HOOOOOOOOOOOOOWL!

From the other side of the mountain, a blood-curdling howl sung out, then another and another. Whatever animal was making them was coming up from the opposite direction. Toby staggered to his feet, pulling his jacket closely around him, and left the cave.

"Toby!" Tash cried out. "Don't leave me!"

"Don't worry – I'm not going far. I need to see what's happening!" He pulled his binoculars out of his pocket. Wedged up against the boulder at the mouth of the cave, he squinted through the glasses. Just at that moment, the clouds raced away from the moon leaving its pale silver light glinting on the side of the mountain. Toby's insides curled. Racing across the snow-covered boulders were a dozen or so dogs, and they were headed straight for him. He froze to the spot.

The dogs! I can't fight them off – but if I go back inside the cave it'll lead them to Tash! What shall I do?

20. Return of the Warrior

"Toby!" Tash called from inside the cave. "What's going on?"

Toby didn't reply. The dogs were racing nearer and nearer. In a few seconds they would be on him.

He closed his eyes and braced himself, then felt a whoosh of air as something leapt over his head. There was a noise of growling and snapping and the gnashing of teeth. He opened his eyes to see a swirl of grey bodies flying past him to collide with the black dogs running towards him.

The wolves! This must be their territory!

The grey and black bodies flung themselves at each other. Some of the dogs were burled over by the fast-moving wolves, their bodies entwined at they hurtled down the mountainside, locked in deadly combat. Toby clung to the boulder, scared to move as around him the animals snapped and bit at each other, their long white fangs dripping with blood.

I'd better not stay here – come on, Toby – GO! If I get back inside whoever wins this battle might forget I am here.

He slowly backed into the cave, gesturing to Tash to keep quiet. Her eyes opened wide in surprise, but she nodded to show she understood. Toby knelt beside the mouth of the cave, clutching a folding walking stick that Tash had found on their way up the mountain.

I might be able to stop one dog or wolf that tries to enter but what if they all attack at the same time?

From outside he could hear the yelps and squeals of the fight. What was going to be the outcome of this battle? What would be better for them – the wolves winning? They might still attack humans when they'd seen the dogs off their territory. Toby glanced at Tash huddled on the ground; he knew they wouldn't be able to make a bid to escape while the fighting was in full flow. She was walking nowhere.

"Toby!" cried Tash, pointing at the entrance. The head and shoulders of a large black dog were filling the mouth of the cave. The dog growled menacingly and bared its sharp gleaming teeth as blood dripped from its mouth.

"GET OUT!" Toby screamed, jabbing towards the dog with the walking stick. But it started to advance slowly, swinging its large slobbering head from side to side. Toby jabbed harder, hastily reversing back into the cave wall. He was stuck now: there was nowhere else to go and still the dog kept coming.

"LEAVE US ALONE!" he shouted. He could smell the dog's evil breath.

"Take that!" cried Tash, throwing the billycan of boiling water at the dog. The water sprayed across its face, burning the tender skin on its muzzle. The dog yelped and momentarily backed off, shaking its head and rubbing its nose with a paw. Now it was an angry dog and, snapping its huge teeth, it sprang forward at Toby. As Toby withdrew into as tight a ball as he could, the flailing teeth sailed past his ankle. The dog, its teeth gnashing with frustration, went to leap again but something stopped it. It screamed in pain and fury; something was attacking it from behind and had grabbed its rump. The dog was being slowly dragged out of the cave, its paws threshing wildly as it attempted to gain a foothold. It tried to bite at whatever had hold of it, its jaws snapping savagely in the air, but there wasn't room for it to turn in the narrow cave entrance. Despite his frantic struggle, the dog slowly disappeared. Toby heard more growling and snarling outside the cave and then there was silence.

"What happened?" asked Tash.

"A wolf must have got him," replied a shocked Toby, still curled up against the cave wall. "Just hope it's not coming back for us next!"

At that, a large, grey, grizzled head appeared in the cave entrance. Toby snatched up his waking stick again and waved it at the wolf.

"No Toby! Don't! It's Snowy!" cried Tash.

"Are you sure? All wolves look the same to me!" Toby gawped at the bright blue eyes staring at him.

"Look – he's still got my pink cream on his paw! Snowy? Snowy – come and say hello," encouraged Tash, holding out her hand to the wolf. The animal lowered his head submissively and squirmed up to Tash, licking at her face, his tail beating out his happiness.

"Yuk! Is that wise?" said Toby. "He might bite your nose off."

"Rubbish, eh, Snowy?"

Once Tash had made a fuss of him, the wolf lay down at the mouth of the cave, his ears pricked, staring into the outer darkness.

"Seems to have gone dead quiet," said Toby. "But maybe the rest of the wolves are outside waiting for us. Maybe they sent Snowy in to lure us out?"

"Do you really believe those wolves are able to think like that?"

"Well, the dogs seem to be able to plan ahead – why are they following us otherwise? It can't be a coincidence they turned up here. Lucky for us the wolves were keen to protect their territory." Toby glanced over at Tash's pale face, but her eyes were closed shut and her lips were turning a funny blue colour.

Oh no, she really looks ill. How am I going to get her out of here to somewhere warm and safe? I can't carry her down the mountain, even if the wolves and dogs have gone.

There was no choice. They had to stay holed up in the cave, at least until daylight when he would be able to see whether it was safe to go out.

As the temperature plummeted in the night, Toby cuddled up to the now sleeping Tash and watched the snow falling outside. Thick white flakes blew horizontally across the mouth of the cave, quickly filling the hole with deep drifts. Snowy had curled up at Tash's feet though Toby was careful not to go too close to him. While the wolf seemed to have bonded to Tash, Toby wasn't sure Snowy would feel the same way about him.

We're going to get snowed in here overnight. What was it the climbers did to make sure that they had enough air in a snow hole? Didn't they stick a pole or something through the roof?

He picked up the walking stick and slid it into the snow so that it poked outside.

Toby pulled all the bags and rucksacks round Tash and huddled next to her, hoping that she would be better by the morning.

Something was licking Toby's nose. Whatever it was, it had hot smelly breath. When Toby woke and opened his eyes, he saw a black-and-white collie wagging his tail furiously at him.

"Monty?"

For a moment Toby thought that he was still in a dream and that his old dog, Monty, had come. This collie stood and cocked his head sideways at Toby.

WOOF!

"Where have you come from? What's your name? Ouch!" Toby tried to move but the cold seemed to have frozen the blood in his legs. The cave was bathed in a strange blue light as a torch outside filtered through the hard-packed ice that now blocked the entrance.

"Tash! Wake up! Someone's here!" Toby cried, shaking the still form lying next to him. On the other side of her lay Snowy, guardedly watching with his hackles raised and his blue eyes staring at the intruder. The collie stood on Toby to reach over and sniff the large shaggy wolf, his tail wagging enthusiastically.

What did Jamie once say about dogs' wagging tails? If they wag fast and horizontally then it's a good sign, and if they wag slow and upright, it's not?

Toby anxiously watched Snowy's reaction as the wolf sniffed back at the collie. Snowy's tail started to wag slowly, brushing the dirt on the floor of the cave. Suddenly he stood up, his huge body filling the tiny space.

"It's ok, Snowy," whispered Tash. "He won't hurt us. He's one of the good dogs."

Reassured by the sound of Tash's voice, Snowy's tail started to wag faster and faster, and he stretched out his neck to lick the collie's ears.

Phew! That could have been nasty! Snowy's obviously used to pet dogs. Thank goodness Tash is awake.

"HELLO?" A man's voice called from outside the cave. "HELLO?"

WOOF! barked the dog again, nudging Toby's hand as if saying he should answer the man, who was now peering in through a small hole in the snow.

"Hello, who are you?" called Toby.

"That's Casper you've got with you. He's a rescue dog. He's the one that found you. Now sit tight and we'll have you dug out in a jiffy!" said the voice.

Who is that? And did he say "we"?

Tash opened one eye and mumbled,

"Raiders? Is it the raiders?"

"I don't think so. I don't know, but he sounds ok..."

"What did he say?"

"They're digging us out. Maybe it's going to be all right." Toby laughed as Casper shook himself and they were splattered with wet globules of ice and snow. "Oh, Casper! Am I glad to see you!" The collie wagged his tail and licked Toby's nose again with his big sloppy tongue.

"Yuk!" Toby patted the dog hard. "You silly boy!"

There was digging and burrowing in the snow at the cave entrance and within a few minutes, a face and then a head and then shoulders, followed by a body, appeared. The man wriggled in, pushing a torch in front of him.

"Hi, my name's Tom, and who are you?"

"I'm Toby and that's Tash, but she's poorly. I don't know what's the matter with her but I'm sure it's not red fever. She did have a rash, but..." Toby babbled on, telling Tom about how they had got there, the trouble with the raiders and how they had lost the spooked ponies. Tash lay curled in a tight sleepy ball, with Snowy standing guard over her.

"Ok, Toby, calm down and don't worry. You're safe now. It's going to be ok. Let's get you both out of here first."

"How did you know we were here?"

"We knew that someone was out here after some ponies with bridles came down off the moor yesterday, so we came looking. Lucky for you, Casper here picked up your scent." The collie bounded up to the man and started licking his face.

"Crikes! What's that?" said Tom, looking at Snowy.

"That's Snowy," replied Toby. "We rescued him at Kingshouse, and then he came and saved our lives. We can't leave him here: the dogs might get him. Can we take him with us?"

"Dogs? We haven't seen any dogs," said Tom. "There are wolves in these mountains but they're completely wild. That's why I'm surprised to see one sitting here! Don't think we can take a wolf with us."

"I'm not going without Snowy!" whispered Tash hoarsely. "And he's not a real wolf – he's a wolf hybrid and he was a pet once. He saved our lives. We can't leave him."

"Ok, ok. He can run alongside the skidoos. He'll have to keep up though," said Tom.

Just then another face appeared at the hole, and then another and another. There seemed to be a crowd outside waiting for them to appear. Toby could hear the sound of spades hitting the icy snow and grunts from the men as they dug fast and furiously. Soon the hole was big enough for them to carry Tash out of the cave, wrapped in a shiny foil blanket. Snowy stood nervously beside her as four men lifted her carefully onto the waiting stretcher, strapping her in tightly.

"It's ok, Snowy," soothed Toby. "They aren't hurting her."

"I don't feel so good," murmured Tash, as the men loaded the stretcher onto the back of a skidoo. Toby squeezed her cold blue hand.

"You're going to be all right now," he reassured her. "These guys have got some serious equipment. We've been saved. Everything's going to be fine."

And maybe these guys can help me on my journey to Stirling? I need to get there, and quick!

21. The Bunker

Toby stood shivering in the dark and cold while the men bustled busily around outside the cave. As their flashing torchlight swept over him, he searched for signs of the battle that had raged between the dogs and the wolves. There was nothing to see but the outlines of the black craggy mountains with the sun starting to rise over them.

"Get on!" yelled Tom, pointing to the back of a skidoo. Toby clambered tiredly on behind one of the men driving, and hung on to his thick waist. Casper jumped up in front of another man, who tucked him into his jacket. The skidoos set off down the steep snowy mountain, with Snowy running alongside the one that carried Tash.

Help! I might have enjoyed this on a nice sunny day, but now I just want to be safe and warm.

The skidoos moved fast along the snow, bouncing and rocketing down the precipitous gully, their headlights sweeping the white ice to the front. Sometimes they skidded sideways to avoid large boulders in the way, sending Toby's stomach lurching. He couldn't see where they were going in the dark, and the freezing wind chilled his face, setting it into a frozen mask. He began to think he would never be able to smile again.

Eventually the skidoos pulled up outside a pair of tall metal gates at the entrance of what looked to Toby like a country park. A large notice was attached to the gates and, in the beams of the headlights, Toby could make out the words:

KEEP OUT – DANGER!
PROPERTY OF THE MINISTRY OF DEFENCE.

The gates swung open and the skidoos stormed through into an area that had once been mown parkland. They sped across the snow-covered grass and stopped in a large yard. Toby couldn't see any buildings as he peered into the darkness.

Where are we now? What is this?

The men got off the vehicles and undid Tash's stretcher. Toby and Snowy were following behind when suddenly the men in front disappeared.

Where have they gone to?

"Down here!" a gruff voice shouted. Toby made out a large concrete ramp descending to an enormous pair of metal doors set in the snowy ground. One of the men spoke into an entry phone and the doors slid slowly back to reveal a stairway going down into the bowels of the earth. The men carefully manoeuvred the stretcher round the bends and corners as the stairs wound deeper and deeper. Toby kept up beside them, leaning heavily on the hand railing. His tired legs still ached and his foot was sore. Snowy trotted quietly along in his shadow, never letting Tash out of his sight.

At the bottom of the stairs was a corridor. They seemed to be in a giant underground bunker.

Is the army hiding down here? Is the government running this place? I wonder how big it is? How many people are down here?

At the end of the corridor, one of the men typed a series of numbers into an entry lock, and a heavy metal door clicked open. They stepped into a large room full of equipment. Toby stared around; it was stashed with hand guns and rifles, rocket launchers, grenade launchers, magazines of ammunition, boxes of shells, alongside helmets, stab vests and camouflage suits in grey, white and mottled green. He could now see that the men were wearing winter camouflage: white suits with white boots, helmets, gloves, goggles and rucksacks.

These are no ordinary mountain rescuers. This looks like the SAS or something.

Tash was whisked away. Tom, seeing Toby looking worried as the stretcher disappeared, said,

"Don't worry, Toby, we have a doctor and he'll know what's wrong with her. We have medicine and anything else she might need. And Snowy can go along, too."

"This place is fantastic!" exclaimed Toby, relaxing a little and staring around him. "You've even got electricity down here!"

"Yes, part of the bunker is based inside a hydro-electric dam so we've our own electricity supply. We'd better get you warmed up. Go with Simon here and he'll sort you out."

Simon showed Toby into a small warm room lined with lockers, and handed him a pile of dry clothes and a towel. He pointed to a cubicle at the back,

"Get yourself cleaned up, son. There's a shower over there. Come back through when you're ready."

Toby slumped onto a bench and peeled off his cold wet clothes. His head throbbed, his feet throbbed and he had a large angry bruise on his knee where Daisy had kicked him.

I look and feel a right mess and I don't smell too good! And I'm starving. Seems ages since I last ate. Wonder what they've got to eat here? But I still need to keep my wits about me and think about how to get to Dad and Sylvie in Stirling.

He stood in the shower for ages, letting the hot water pummel his aching body until he was warmed through. He'd to scrub hard with the soap to get rid of the layers of grime that stuck to his skin, and was surprised to see how pink he was under all the muck. Then he dressed in the man-sized clean clothes, which hung limply from his scrawny frame.

Back in the main room, Toby found Tom staring at a large map of central Scotland pinned to a desk.

"That's better, Toby. Now, you must be starving – go and help yourself to something hot over there." He pointed to a canteen area at the back of the huge room. There were tables and chairs set out. Simon came with him to show him what there was.

"Good grub…" said Toby, his mouth stuffed full of hot creamy porridge. There was chunky vegetable soup, drop scones, oatcakes, scrambled eggs, bowls of jam, and tinned peaches.

"Take it steady," said Simon. "Don't go overdoing it. Don't want to make yourself sick."

Toby nodded, biting into a warm, jammy scone.

Later, warm and full, Toby wandered over to the map table where several of the men, including Tom and Simon, stood chatting.

"So Toby," said Tom, "it was good thinking on your part to stick that walking pole out of your snow hole. You might have suffocated if you hadn't. And it was the pole that Casper smelt out, so well done you."

"My dad told me that," smiled Toby.

Would Dad be proud of me remembering that? I saved us! Well – Casper helped too.

"You said before, Toby," said Simon, "that you were heading towards Stirling. Why's that then?"

"That's where New Caledonia is."

I'm surprised they haven't heard about it. It can't be far from here, surely?

"So, Toby, what do you know about this New Caledonia?" asked another of the men. This man had a dark unsmiling face, and he stared with cold unflinching eyes, as if he didn't believe what Toby was telling them.

I don't like him. He looks as bad as the raiders.

"I don't know anything, honest. I just want to get my dad and my little sister, Sylvie, back from the raiders. I... I just..." Toby almost burst into tears. It was bad enough to deal alone with cold, soreness, terrible worry and disappointment, to then be disbelieved and mistrusted by people he'd thought were the good guys was simply too much.

"It's ok, Toby," said Tom kindly, "You'll have to forgive Bill, he's used to interrogating terrorists and the like. Give the boy a break, Bill. He's been through some serious stuff and come out of it very well by all accounts."

"I do know that the place is run by someone called the General," said Toby, wondering if telling them more might help his dad and Sylvie. "I met his Captain, who was scary enough, but all the raiders were seriously terrified of this General bloke. And I know he's kidnapping people but I've no idea why. I mean, what would he want with my dad and Sylvie?"

"He's a nasty piece of work," said Simon. "You wouldn't want to cross him."

"Yeah," said Bill. "He's got no scruples when it comes to torturing people to find out what he needs to know."

"Torturing people? To find out what?" cried Toby. Was the General torturing his dad right now? "What do you mean?"

"He's set up his own state," continued Bill. "He's collecting up survivors to do the dirty work for him so that he and his private army can live in luxury while he starves the…"

"I think Toby's heard enough, eh, Toby?" interrupted Tom, scowling at Bill. "We don't want to frighten him, do we, Bill?"

Bit late for that! As if I'm not already worried about Dad and Sylvie —now I find out that the General is probably torturing and starving them.

"Just tell me one thing," pleaded Toby, fighting hard to hold back his tears. "What sort of information would the General be trying to get out of my dad?"

"We think he's probably running out of fuel," said Tom, putting his hand on Toby's arm. "He'll be looking at different ways to make electricity – like putting up wind turbines or solar panels. It's unlikely that he's got anyone there who knows anything about those sorts of things. What he needs is an engineer."

"Oh! My dad's an engineer!" blurted out Toby.

"In that case, he'll be very useful to the General. If your dad chooses to cooperate with him, he should be fine," said Tom reassuringly.

"And what if he doesn't want to cooperate?" asked Toby, feeling his face redden. The men looked away: Toby could see that wasn't something they wanted to discuss.

Great! I can't imagine Dad going along with the plans of some mad man!

Toby didn't want to hear any more.

"Can I go and see Tash now?" He rubbed his hot face on the nice new jumper they had given him.

Simon showed him to the emergency room, where Tash was lying, propped up on a pile of clean pillows. She had a pink glow to her like she had been scrubbed clean. Beside the bed was a drip-stand with a line going into a pad on her arm. Snowy was lying nearby on the floor, tucking into a large bowl of porridge.

"Look Tobes!" she called, on seeing him pop his head round the door. "I've got medicine going straight into my arm! I'm feeling much better already."

Toby smiled. She did look so much better. He sat for a while and chatted, but he could soon see that she needed to sleep. As he left, the doctor came over to speak to him.

"What was wrong with her?" asked Toby.

"Your friend has been very lucky. She had an impacted tooth that had been festering away for some time. It became infected and naturally made her really poorly. She was very sick when she came in. I extracted the tooth immediately, so she'll feel much better now. Also, we've got her on some intravenous antibiotics, which will kill any infection. She'll be right as rain in a few days time."

Thank goodness for that! Poor Tash – there was I calling her moody and all the time she had serious toothache. How awful. Why didn't she tell me?

But Toby knew why – Tash was trying to prove that she was as brave as Toby could be. She wouldn't have wanted to moan in case he'd thought she was a sissy.

Silly Tash. I would never have thought that.

Toby sat down suddenly as his legs buckled under him.

Now he had been relieved of some of his worries, he was overwhelmed with exhaustion.

"Come on, young man, looks like you need some care and attention, too," said the doctor, helping him to a nearby bed. Toby smiled weakly and then passed out.

22. Red-Hot Anger

"So, young man," a voice boomed in Toby's ear. "How are you feeling today?"

Toby opened his eyes and wriggled up in his pillows to see Tom standing next to his bed, gazing at him.

"Eh? Fine, I think," Toby rubbed his eyes and yawned. "Where is this?"

"You're in the medical bay," replied Tom.

"No, I mean, what is this place? Where is it? And who are you and all these men? Have you been here all the time since the red fever?"

"What a lot of questions! I tell you what, I'll give you a guided tour and explain as we go along," said Tom. "Get dressed and I'll come back for you."

Good – I need to see what they've got here. Then I can work out how to get to Stirling, and whether they might even help me.

Ten minutes later Tom escorted Toby around the underground bunker, showing him all the facilities. Toby was amazed to see that not only was there a kitchen, sleeping quarters, offices, a canteen and a medical bay, but there was also a gym, a games room, a library and a huge garage for maintaining a fleet of vehicles. There was even a laboratory where two young women in white protective suits were peering down microscopes.

"That's our experimental unit," Tom told him. "We're trying to work out why some people were immune to red fever, and others weren't."

As they walked round the vast compound, Toby told Tom the story of his dad and Sylvie being kidnapped by the raiders, following them to Fort George, meeting Tash, and then how he and Tash had fled just as the dogs attacked.

"There were hundreds of dogs. Some had been following me along the coast, and they must have told the others about Fort George..." But Toby could see Tom didn't believe him.

"Really? Sounds strange. I'm amazed the dogs got into Fort George. I used to be stationed there years ago, so I know what a strong fortress it is," said Tom thoughtfully.

"Cerberus is so cunning and clever he could get in anywhere."

"Cerberus? This is the dog you claim is leading the others to attack places? Well, I'm not sure about that, Toby."

"You don't know Cerberus. Jamie's mum called him that 'cause he's so evil, and he's clever and she thinks —"

"Ok, so Jamie's mum, whoever she is, thinks this dog is clever. But we know a dog is just a dog don't we, Toby?"

"But Cerberus is different. You've no idea what he's capable of!" cried Toby, defiantly.

"No – and I don't think I want to!" Tom laughed. "You've had a very adventurous time, Toby, and I expect a very stressful one too. Stress can do funny things to you, makes you imagine things. You'll see things in a different light once you've had a rest and feel safe again."

Toby blushed.

I haven't made it up! It did all happen! Why do adults never believe me?

"Have you seen any dogs?" he asked, trying to hide his disappointment. If Tom and his men didn't believe him, how could they help him find his family and keep them all safe – from the dogs as well as the raiders.

"Dogs? No, no dogs. We've only seen the wolves that have been breeding in the mountains. There are a lot of those now. Besides, I thought you said all the dogs were at Fort George? They couldn't possibly have got this far south so quickly!"

Oh yes, they could have.

Just then the scary-looking man, Bill, strode up to Tom.

"You'd better come – we have some new information just in."

Tom nodded and left Toby to find his own way back to the medical bay. Toby found Tash sitting in bed reading a book, with Snowy lying near her feet.

"Look what the doctor found for me: a Russian book!" she said excitedly, holding it up for Toby to see.

"Yeah, great isn't it? They've got a library full of all sorts of books. It's an amazing place, Tash. There's a lab where they're doing experiments, and a gym, and the hugest garage with loads of tools to mend stuff. And..."

"But what is it all for?"

"Tom says this was a Scottish base for one of the SAS regiments, sort of covert undercover operations and all that. It's been here for years, long before the red fever."

"Like in James Bond?"

"Er, that kind of idea. Anyway, some of the men from the regiment survived the red fever and came back here. They've been gathering intelligence on the effects of the illness on Scotland, and seeing who's left."

"So why haven't they got soldiers' names then?"

"What? You mean like Tom's not called a Major or Captain? Well, Tom says that there are only a few real soldiers. Most of the people who stay here now are civilians: engineers, scientists, mechanics, teachers – about fifty altogether."

"Does Tom know all about the raiders?"

"Tom told me last night that the General is creating a new state where he'll be in charge and live in luxury. I've told him about the dogs and Cerberus, but he doesn't believe me. They have seen loads of wolves. I bet it was wolves we heard when the ponies got spooked and took off."

"I've never seen ponies so scared," she sighed wistfully. Toby could see she had been blaming herself for losing the ponies.

"I'm going back to sleep now. I still feel a bit yuk." Tash yawned.

Toby went to look for Tom.

He found him looking serious, talking to a group of men including Simon and Bill. The men all appeared fit: tall and well muscled. They were talking enthusiastically about going on a job.

What job? Where are they planning to go? They look like they're kitted out for a mission.

The men were wearing their winter camouflage gear again, with white snowsuits on and goggles slung round their necks. As Toby approached they fell quiet and stared at the map on the desk. He followed their gaze and realised that the area around Stirling had been circled in red pen, and there were arrows marking a route.

"So you know exactly where New Caledonia is?" asked Toby bravely. He sounded much bolder than he felt.

Tom frowned at him and Toby thought for one moment he was going to get a row, but Tom's face softened and he said,

"Yes, Toby, we know all about the activities of the General, we've been spying on him and his New Caledonia for months. Give him his due, he's intelligent, well organised and he must have some charm to be able to persuade the others to do what he says. He's made a good job of fortifying the boundaries of his new country. We've been planning a mission for a while now —"

"Can I come?" Toby blurted out. A couple of the men laughed.

"I'm sorry. It does sound likely that they have your family, and I realise you must be very worried about them. But let us handle it – these men are trained professionals. They know what they're doing."

"But I can be useful. I know things about the raiders," said Toby, trying to keep Tom's attention. "For instance, the General's henchmen all have a special tattoo on their wrists, just here." Toby pulled back his sleeve and pointed to the place where he had seen /NC on the men's arms.

"Thank you. That'll be useful in identifying the raiders, but I'm afraid I still can't take you. I can't jeopardise a mission." Tom turned on his heels and strode off.

The guy called Bill smirked, but Simon came over and put a hand on Toby's shoulder.

"Sorry, Toby, it isn't your age. We never take untrained civilians, ok?"

Toby shook his head, and then felt a red-hot surge of anger.

How dare these men treat me like a baby? After all the scary things I've had to do. Who rescued Jamie and his mum, and who got me and Tash this far?

He took a deep breath; falling out with Simon wasn't going to help his cause. He'd have to be more cunning than that. "So are you going to go in all guns blasting then?" he asked, trying to sound innocent.

"Absolutely not," replied Simon, stooping to hide the map from Toby's curious eyes. "It'll be a stealth operation: quick in and out."

"How are you going to rescue all the people that fast?"

"We're not. We're only going to bring out the General and his henchmen – just the ringleaders. It'll be easier now you've told us about the tattoos – we'll be able to identify them quicker."

Toby felt the anger rear its ugly head again and this time he couldn't help blurting out, "But what about my dad and Sylvie? You're going to leave them there? You can't do that. They're prisoners. You need to rescue them! That's what you do, isn't it? Rescue people? You rescued me so why can't you rescue them?" Toby's voice was getting louder and louder and a few people in the canteen were starting to stare. Simon took him by his arm and led him out into the corridor.

"I'm really sorry about your family, Toby," he said, "but they'll be safer this way. We haven't got the firepower or the trained men to take on the General in a full-scale attack. You heard what Tom said: the General's been careful to protect his territory. It would be a suicide mission. Lots of innocent people could get injured and you don't want that, do you?"

Toby shook his head.

"This way," continued Simon, "we take out the worst of the raiders and the place will soon fall apart. From our observations, we know that most of the men are not hardened criminals. Most of them just seem to have fallen in with bad company to survive. We remove the bad company and hopefully the others will behave in a civilised way again and let the innocent people live freely."

"Hopefully?" exclaimed Toby. "What do you mean hopefully? And what if they don't?"

"Then we'll have to think again, won't we? Toby, we can't rescue everybody anyway. This place won't support any more people. We're at full capacity as it is now and all those here came by invitation because they have some special knowledge."

"What?" cried Toby. He saw in his face that Simon hadn't meant to tell him that. Simon shrugged and walked away, muttering something about it being a hard world and there were things that just had to be done.

They don't want to rescue Dad and Sylvie. They've known for ages that the General has been kidnapping people and torturing them. Tom doesn't want anyone else here. How can he leave the prisoners at the mercy of those men? Even if the bad guys aren't there, who knows what will happen? I'm going to have to rescue them myself.

Toby raced back to his room in the medical bay. His clothes had been washed and dried and were now in a locker beside the bed. He pulled them on quickly, then, throwing his rucksack over his shoulder, he slipped out into the corridor.

They are not going without me! I'm going to Stirling and they can't stop me.

He realised that they could, and they would if they caught him trying to go with them.

They must be leaving soon – they were all kitted up. Maybe if I find out which vehicle they are going in, I could stow away in it?

This didn't sound like a very good plan; the chances of being able to hide from professional soldiers seemed slim.

Haven't had a chance to say goodbye to Tash. I hope she's not going to be too mad I'm going without her, but I've got to do this.

23. New Caledonia

Toby crept quietly down a corridor heading to the huge garage he had seen with Tom, trying hard to remember where he was in the vast bunker. Suddenly he froze; he could hear someone angrily shouting and a banging noise coming from somewhere nearby. He listened again. One of the voices seemed familiar. Sliding round the corner, Toby peered through the window of what seemed like a prison cell. There inside, banging with a metal cup on the wall, was Carl, the driver of the Land Rover Toby had taken.

Carl? How did he get here?

Toby bobbed under the window and sneaked a look inside the next cell. There, on a narrow metal bed, sat the driver of the white van, looking very pleased as he gobbled up a large plate of hot pie and chips.

"Eh – you? It's you! You wee maggot!" Carl had come to his window and spied Toby. "I know you!" he shouted. "You're the wee toad that stole my Landie. If I get my hands on you, you'll be sorry you ever set eyes on that truck!"

Toby didn't wait to reply but sped on up the corridor and through a metal door into the garage. It was more like a small aircraft hangar with its tall curved roof and big doors at the bottom end. Toby crouched in the shadow of a large lorry, watching out for men. There were mainly green army Land Rovers parked alongside the skidoos, but also there were a couple of big lorries, and a white van.

The white van? That must be Carl's mate's van, the one we were following from Fort William. Why have they captured that?

Just then, two of the soldiers appeared out of a side door, and slung a couple of bags into the open back of the van.

They must be taking the van on the mission. That's clever! They'll be using it to get inside this New Caledonia place, to fool the guards.

Two other soldiers appeared and got into one of the green Land Rovers, banging the doors shut. Toby heard the noise of an engine starting.

They must be leaving – I'd better get going.

He ducked and dived behind the lorries and trucks until he reached the white van and then, glancing around him, jumped into the back. Wriggling under a bench seat, Toby pulled an old blanket around him. Now all he had to do was wait.

It seemed like ages as he lay there trying to slow his breathing. Were they taking the van? Or was he going to be left behind? As he was beginning to think that he had made a big mistake, he heard voices. It was Bill and Simon, and they were discussing the route to Stirling. One man got into the cab of the van and the door slammed shut. The engine revved into life and they started to move. There was the sound of the huge metal doors opening, and then the van picked up speed.

Toby's stomach lurched as the van headed up a ramp, bumping him around in the back. He was on the way to Stirling now.

Bright winter sunlight flooded in through the rear window. Toby hadn't realised what time of day it was; it was easy to lose all track of time in the bunker. Judging by the lowness of the light, it was early afternoon. It would soon be dark.

Toby began to feel sick, as the driver threw the van around corners and raced along the country lanes at speed. He tried to think of a plan for when he arrived at New Caledonia but he couldn't concentrate. He braced himself against the struts of the bench, holding his breath with every lurch and bump, scared that the driver might hear him gasping.

What am I going to do? How am I going to find Dad and Sylvie? And what will I do when I've found them?

The journey seemed to go on and on forever, but just when Toby thought his stomach wouldn't be able to take much more, they lurched to a halt. He heard muffled voices calling out in the dark. The driver wound down his window and shouted something gruffly. The van started up again, slowly moving and then manoeuvring around until it came to a stop and the driver turned the engine off. Toby peeped from under the blanket just in time to see the driver hide the van keys behind the sun visor, before getting out of the van and closing the door quietly. Then there was silence.

Toby lay for a while, wondering what to do. Was it safe to leave the van? Or was there someone out there? He had to take the risk and look. He wriggled out from under the bench, his legs stiff and cramped, then crawled over the front seats and into the driver's place. He peered out of the windscreen into the murky darkness. The van appeared to be parked in a large car park alongside a fleet of lorries and white vans. He could just make out the sentry post they had passed through. Two large men stood with their backs to him, hunched with cold, staring into a fiery brazier burning with coals. As the heat-hazy light threw shadows onto them, Toby could see the AK47 rifles slung over their shoulders.

Where am I? This place looks enormous.

There was no sign of the driver, so Toby got out very carefully and slunk round the back of the van. He realised that he was in the car park of what looked like a huge castle with towering walls and batteries looming up to his left.

This must be Stirling Castle!

He remembered passing the place when he and his family had travelled down to Glasgow to see his grandma. He had wanted to explore the melodramatic castle with its lofty buildings and fortifications, all perched on a huge rocky cliff high above the main road.

There was a large parade ground in front of the castle, leading to the main gateway. He wouldn't be able to get through there as the open ground gave him no cover, and he reckoned there must be guards there, too.

There must be an easier entrance.

The van was parked with its back to a wall in which there was a narrow wrought iron gate swinging off its hinges. Toby crawled along the gravel to the gate and slipped through onto the grass on the other side.

Oh no, a cemetery, and in the dark too.

Toby flashed his torch on. He'd have to take the risk of someone seeing the light; he wasn't brave enough to crawl through a graveyard at night. All around him stood lines of stones sticking up like rows of giant black teeth. Some of the gravestones were decorated on top with Celtic crosses, urns, and one even had a huge angel, wings aloft, staring down at him with empty eyes. He moved quickly through the broken ground, tripping over tussocks of long grass in his haste to get out of the cemetery.

I'll go round the back of the castle. There may be an entrance there that's not guarded. After all, Cerberus managed to find a way into Fort George.

Toby stopped and held his breath. Could he hear something snuffling about in the bushes beside the wall? No, he must be imagining it. He started slowly picking his way round a stone slab which had slipped off a grave and lay crookedly across the grass.

Hope the person inside doesn't fall out, too!

"AH!" Toby screamed. A large gloved hand grabbed him by the shoulder. Out of the darkness stepped a short thick-set man in a black balaclava and dark clothes.

"Got yer!" he cried. "Yer coming with me!"

The man twisted Toby's arm behind his back and marched him, stumbling, back across the cemetery to the main entrance of the castle. They passed across a dry moat and under an archway, the man's head-torch bobbing a light in front of them. At the other side of another bridge sat a large stone gatehouse from which light spilled onto the flagged pavement. The man threw Toby roughly to the ground.

"What yer gone and caught this time, Bert?" someone called out from inside the gatehouse.

"Looks like a minnow to me!" called another. Laughter spilt out into the night. Toby kept his face down because he didn't want to be recognised; some of these men might have seen him at Fort George. But then he heard a voice he knew.

"Wait! Let me have a good look at him!" It was the Captain of the raiders. He tugged Toby's head up by his hair. "That's the lad who got away from us and nicked McNaught's boat, too. He was furious. Think you've just used up another of your lives, cat-boy!"

The other men roared with laughter and came out of the guardhouse to get a better look at this lad with nine lives, who had dared to do such things.

"Take him straight to the General. He'll be very interested to meet this one. Maybe he can use him to get his dad to talk!" barked the Captain. Two men dragged Toby across a large sloping courtyard towards an arch bridging the corner. This had a crenellated roof and gothic windows in its side. Peering out of one of the windows, caught in the glimmering lights of the men's torches, was a small pale face encircled with fair gossamer hair.

Jamie!

"Get a move on!" one of the men grunted at him, pushing him roughly. They climbed up a cobbled ramp and were in another courtyard. To their right stood a massive pale-gold hall decorated with statues and lots of fancy plasterwork. The men pushed Toby through a huge wooden door. The Great Hall was even more magnificent inside, with hundreds of large candles shimmering against the creamy white walls, casting flickering patterns of light and dark into the wooden beams of the vaulted ceiling.

Candles. They haven't got any electricity left.

Toby winced as one of the men grabbed his arm. At the end of the hall, sitting in a large wooden throne was an even larger man.

That must be the General! What a size he is! And what is he wearing?

Toby was thrust forward to fall at the foot of the throne. He stared up at a very strange sight. The huge ugly man had on a pillar-box red military uniform emblazoned on the chest with dozens of badges, insignia, and a whole rainbow of coloured strips of cloth, like those given as medals to war heroes.

Bet he's never even been in the army!

Huge silver epaulettes hung from the General's shoulders and slung across his body was a silk tasselled lanyard in brilliant white. He wore a large peaked hat, which was also covered in badges. He looked like he was about to go on parade.

Wow! What a sight! Think he fancies himself as the dictator of Scotland!

"So what do we have here?" snapped the General, gazing down at Toby as if he had just crawled out from under a stone. Toby could now see that the man had a large scar down one side of his face that pulled his right eye down as if it were half closed. It gave him an almost funny look, but Toby wasn't laughing; the General looked mean.

"It's Mr Tennant's son, sir," said the thickset man who had now removed his balaclava to reveal an ugly trout-like face. He puckered up his flabby lips and squinted at Toby. "He's the one that got away when we kidnapped his dad and sister. Then he caught up with us at Fort George and set the dogs on us. And after he'd led the dogs' attack he scarpered in McNaught's speedboat."

"Well, boy? You led dogs to attack my fort!" yelled the General. "Do you realise that attack has cost me our foothold in the north? How am I going to rule Scotland if every time we set foot outside New Caledonia, my men get set upon by wild dogs? And it seems you are their leader!"

"WHAT?" Toby gathered himself together. "I never led the dogs anywhere. They were led by Cerberus, coming from Aberdeen. And Fort George wasn't your fort anyway. Your men stole it from the families living there. And come to think of it where are those people? AND WHERE'S MY DAD AND MY LITTLE SISTER?"

By this time the men were laughing at Toby as he stood up with his chest puffed out trying to look as tall and menacing as possible.

Someone cuffed him on the back of the head and he fell back down.

"Don't dare speak to the General like that!" cried the trout-face, lashing out at Toby with his boot.

"So, what can you tell me about your dad, then?" asked the General, leaning forward to fix Toby with a belligerent stare from his lop-sided eyes.

"I'm not telling you anything," stammered Toby.

"Oh, but you will. You wouldn't want anything to happen to that sweet little sister of yours, would you?"

"You wouldn't hurt Sylvie?"

"I won't have to if you just tell me what your dad's job was. You see, we need people with knowledge to help run my new country. We must have scientists, doctors and engineers – people with skills so that we can build a new world. But I need power! We can't exist forever foraging for the scattered fuel dumps that remain. I need someone to design me some way of making electricity, and I think your dad might just be that someone."

"Why? What makes you think that? My dad was an —" Toby was just about to tell when he realised that he had fallen right into the General's trap. "I'm not telling you. If he wouldn't then neither can I!"

"Please yourself, laddie! I'm going to enjoy this. You and your dad – sooner or later one of you will talk. We'll see whose pips squeak first, shall we?"

There was a chorus of agreement from the men who then roared with laughter.

Please don't let them torture me! I mustn't tell them about the bunker and that Tom and his men are about to attack at any moment!

24. The General

Toby lay curled in a tight ball on the floor, anticipating a sharp kick from one of the raiders. Suddenly the General leapt to his feet clutching his head. He towered over Toby, his huge frame dwarfing everyone around him.

Crikey! He must be about seven feet tall. No wonder they're all scared of him.

"QUIET! I must have quiet! Ah! My head!" he screamed, in obvious agony. The men hurriedly backed away.

This isn't the first time he's done this, judging by their reaction. What's the matter with him? One minute he was ok and the next he's a screaming monster.

The General slumped back into his throne and sat rocking back and forth, cradling his head in his hands, and gesticulating for everyone to leave him.

Toby stayed still; he'd had an idea.

"I can help you," he stated bravely, uncurling and standing up. He took a step towards the throne.

"Get away, lad!" barked the Captain, who had just joined them. "The General doesn't need your help."

"Please yourself," said Toby, shrugging and trying hard to look nonchalant.

What am I thinking of? I must be mad! If this doesn't work, I'm dead.

"Shut up!" yelled the Captain, yanking Toby away by his shoulder.

"Don't shout," moaned the General. "Let the boy tell us how he can help."

"Well, in truth, it's not me exactly," started Toby hesitantly. This plan of his could easily go wrong. "I happen to know that you have a talented doctor here and her son, who is a gifted homeopathist. I'm sure they will be able to help you."

"Oh, are you now?" grunted the Captain, sarcastically. "And what's a ho-mop-path-ist?"

"Don't show your ignorance!" the General hissed at the Captain. "I know what a homeopathist is! I'm an educated man, for god's sake! Just as well I am! We'd still be cowering in the caves if it had been left to you!"

Toby turned to the Captain; he needed to get him on his side for this to work. So he explained quietly, "They're like a natural healer. I know they can help 'cause I was dying once of a septic hand and Jamie made me medicine from herbs and plants and I got better straight away. His mum saved my sister, who was dying of red fever."

That's a bit of an exaggeration. Hope he goes for it.

"Is that right?" said the Captain, sneering. "And how do you know these people are here?"

"I've seen them," said Toby, hoping that Jamie's mum was with Jamie.

"What you waiting for? Go and fetch them here, now!" the General snarled at the Captain.

"You'd better come with me," the Captain ordered Toby. "We'll see if we can find these miracle workers!"

The Captain dragged Toby outside and across the large yard to a door, which he unlocked and swung open. In the darkness before him, Toby could hear the murmurings of someone; lots of someones. The Captain shone his torch into another hall, flashing it over rows of blankets lying on the floor. Peering out of the makeshift beds, blinking in the torchlight, were the shocked faces of women and children. Some cried out with fright, while others stared out sullenly; one of those was Jamie's mum.

"Hurry up and find these people that are going to cure the General! He doesn't like to be kept waiting," snarled the Captain. He strode off down the hall to inspect the other prisoners.

"Katie?" Toby couldn't stop himself from yelling out. "Katie, it's Toby. Is Jamie with you? And where's Sylvie?"

"Toby? Toby is that you?" called a familiar voice. A blonde head stuck up from underneath a pile of blankets.

"J-J-Jamie?" Toby's voice broke with relief.

From under another pile of blankets a tousle of brown hair stirred and a small pale face peeped out. "Tobes? Is that really you?"

"Sylvie? Sylvie! Yes! – It's me, Toby!" He gasped with amazement as a small figure stumbled towards him. He picked her up in his arms and hugged her tight, unable to speak, while tears of relief pricked his eyes.

"Oh, Tobes, I'm SO pleased to see you!" sighed Sylvie, wrapping her arms around his neck. "The bad men here are horrid, and one big monster man is really really horrible and was shouting at Dad and me, and —".

"Where's Dad?" Toby anxiously asked her.

"I don't know, Tobes. We were together until we got here and then, after the monster man had shouted at us, they took him away on his own."

Toby put her down and took her hand tightly in his.

"They haven't hurt you have they, Sylve?"

"No, they were a bit rough but I'm ok. I just kept thinking that you'd be here soon to rescue us – and here you are! I knew that you would come. I am very hungry, though!"

"Good, well I'm here now but we need to find Dad, and fast. Here, I've got some cereal bars in my pocket. Take one. They're a bit fusty but it'll stop you being hungry." Toby pushed the squashed packet into Sylvie's hand.

Jamie came stumbling towards him, grabbed him in a big bear hug and burst into tears.

"It's so good to see you!" Jamie stuttered. "Sylvie and I knew you would come!"

"Don't," mumbled Toby, "you'll start me off, and we don't want him to see us crying, do we?" He nodded towards the Captain who came striding up to them.

"So," snapped the Captain. "This is your 'gifted' whatever-he-is. Looks like a cry-baby to me. I hope you're right about him. The General doesn't like being disappointed. And come on, you – if you're the so-called doctor." He motioned for Jamie's mum,

Katie, to come too. She quickly pulled on her clothes and came over, giving Toby a big hug too.

"We're so glad to see you, Toby. We've been really worried about you. How on earth did you manage to find us here?" she said.

"Shut up!" interrupted the Captain. "And get a move on!" He roughly pushed them out of the door and locked it behind him. Toby managed to pull Sylvie out of the door with them in the darkness.

"She's not coming!" barked the Captain.

"She is," Toby yelled back. "Or else your General doesn't get treated by these two." Toby nodded towards Jamie and his mum who both look puzzled. As they returned to the Great Hall he whispered the bare bones of his plan to them. All they had to do was try to treat the General. He had no idea of what they should do after that.

Standing in front of the General's throne, Toby took a good look at Jamie and his mum. They were dressed in filthy blue boiler suits that were much too big for them and only emphasised how thin they had become. They both looked hollow-eyed and tired, their grey faces smeared with mud.

Don't suppose I look that good either. But they look starving. Sylvie doesn't look too bad but she hasn't been here that long.

"So, what is the matter with you?" declared Katie, defiantly marching up to the General. He was still slumped in his throne, clutching his head. "Looks to me like you've got a migraine," she stated loudly. "Are you seeing flashing lights? Do you feel sick?"

"Yeah, all of those," he muttered back. "And keep your voice down, my head's splitting!"

"Jamie, have you got any of those dried pachu berries left in your rucksack?" She turned to her son, who was grasping tight onto Toby's arm.

"Umm, oh, I don't know. Yes, I think so..." he muttered, looking petrified.

"Go and fetch them then. Go on – now!" she ordered. Toby smiled to himself. Katie was great. If she was scared she certainly didn't show it.

My mum was like that, too – really stood up for me when I needed her to.

Toby wasn't sure of the next part of his plan. His first priority had been to get to Jamie and his mum and check they were all right. He hoped that they could cure the General of whatever was wrong with him, and then maybe he would let them go out of gratitude.

"I'm afraid that these migraines will keep coming back..." Katie was saying.

Don't tell him that! We'll never get away.

"...if you don't look after yourself better. Don't drink red wine, avoid rich foods, don't get too stressed, and don't read in a poor light for long."

"Huh! I like my food," grumbled the General. "And I'm not giving up my red wine. All I want from you and that kid of yours is to make the pain go away."

"Right, well, in that case I shall give you some strong painkillers. We'll mix them with dried pachu berries. That will take the pain away, and stop you feeling sick."

"Then get on with it!" howled the General, nursing his head.

Toby waited anxiously with Sylvie while Katie followed Jamie to fetch what they needed from their bags, back in the Palace Hall with the makeshift beds in it. He watched as they mixed up a pink potion of gooey liquid in a mug and gave it to the General.

"You don't expect me to drink this muck, do you?" he cried.

"You can rub it on your baldy head for all I care," retorted Katie. "But if you want that pain to go away, you'll slurp down every last drop."

Toby chuckled. Katie had real fighting spirit.

The General pulled a face like a small child being made to take his medicine, and swallowed the contents of the mug.

"So, can we go now?" asked Katie. "One good turn deserves another."

"No chance! You're going nowhere, and anyway, how do I know that this isn't some rubbish you've given me?"

"Or poison?" suggested the Captain.

"You don't," said Katie. "You'll just have to trust me."

"I don't trust anybody. You're going nowhere. Throw *them* back in with the others. And put *him* in the dungeon with the other one," growled the General, pointing at Toby.

That was a rubbish plan.

One of the raiders grabbed Toby by the scruff of his jacket collar.

"Tobes! Don't leave me!" screamed Sylvie as one of the raiders grabbed her and started to drag her out of the Great Hall with Jamie and Katie.

"Don't worry, Sylvie. I'll find you! Go with Katie and Jamie!" Toby yelled back, his stomach churning.

Stupid of me to think there might be honour among thieves.

25. Sending a Signal

Sylvie, Jamie and Katie were hauled across the dark yard, while the Captain dragged Toby back towards the guardhouse.

"You better pray that your mates' medicine works, else you're up for the high jump, too!" barked the Captain, pulling Toby down a flight of steps to a small wooden door. He unlocked it and threw Toby inside.

Toby waited until the Captain's footsteps disappeared into the night, and then pulled out his torch. Giving it a quick wind-up, he shone it round the dank smelly cell in which he found himself.

"Hello?" he called out. There in the corner lay slumped a figure dressed in dirty jeans and an "Edinburgh Rocks" sweatshirt. The figure groaned and moved.

It couldn't be Dad, could it?

"Dad?" Toby crouched and put his hand out.

"I'm not your dad. It's Captain Bill Gallagher to you, son," croaked a voice.

"Bill? From the bunker? What are you doing here? I thought you were leading an attack?"

"Well, I didn't get very far, did I?"

"What happened?" In the excitement of finding

Sylvie and the others, Toby had forgotten all about the impending attack by the soldiers.

"I got given away by some stupid dog that was hanging around the cemetery. It was following me – wanted to play! When I tried to shoo it off, it started yelping and the guards heard it."

Strange – a friendly dog? Couldn't be one of Cerberus's pack, then.

"Are you hurt?" asked Toby. He could see that the soldier was lying at a funny angle.

"My leg – must have twisted it when those guys jumped me. I was supposed to give a signal to the others once I had got in. My mission was to open the back gates for them. There's no chance of that now."

Toby pulled his rucksack from under his jacket where he had been hiding it.

"I might have something in my bag to help with that," he nodded towards Bill's leg. He set the torch down so that it shone on the rucksack, and started to empty it.

"What's this?" he exclaimed, pulling out a battered, dirty brown teddy bear.

"Ha!" scoffed Bill. "That's going to be a lot of use, isn't it?"

Toby could feel himself going red.

"Hang on, that's not my teddy. This can't be my bag. This is Tash's rucksack. They must have got muddled up somehow at the bunker."

Toby threw all the contents onto the floor and rummaged around. Tash's bag had all sorts of stuff in it. He picked up the penknife and the hacksaw. Maybe those would be useful? Could he file the lock off the door?"

"YES!" he cried out, unearthing a bunch of metal key-like objects from under a tin of tuna. "Tash's skeleton keys! I'd forgotten she had these!"

"Hush!" whispered Bill. "And where did you get those from? They're really rare."

"Never mind that, let's get out of here, now," whispered Toby. He pocketed the penknife and the hacksaw and made for the door. Bill pulled himself up slowly.

"I think I've broken my ankle. You'll have to go without me. What's the plan?"

Toby thought for a moment. He didn't have a plan, he just wanted to find his dad and get them all out of there.

"Em... I'll go and get Jamie and Katie, then I'll... I'll think about it as I go along," he stammered. This didn't look good. Bill must think he was an idiot. "I know, why don't I first go and open the back gates and give the signal, then at least *your* plan can be put into action? I can go back after that for the others."

"You? You open the back gates? How are you going to manage that? You're just a scrawny wee kid."

"I don't know, but we haven't got much choice have we?"

Just a kid? I'll show him who's just a kid.

"Ok, you're right there," sighed Bill. "We haven't got many options at the moment, have we? So, take a right out of here and go through the north gate – it's like a tunnel that comes out into an area called the 'nether bailey'. You'll go by a row of old buildings on your left. Head straight across the grass, keeping the north wall on your right and you'll come to a metal gate in the wall. It used to be blocked up but the raiders have opened it so the workers have easy access to the fields."

"Workers? You mean the people they've kidnapped, don't you?" cried Toby.

He means all those poor women and children in that hall, and the men. But where are they keeping the men? And is Dad with them?

"More or less... But listen carefully, once you have managed to unlock those gates you need to get somewhere high up and use your torch to flash the signal to the west. An SOS will do. You know how to do that, don't you?"

"Yes, I do."

"I'll stay here in case they check on us. You'd better lock the door behind you, and I'll use my jacket to make a pile in the corner. Hopefully in the dark they'll think it's you."

"Ok, I'll come back for you soon. Don't worry," said Toby, in what he hoped was a calm voice.

"I hope so," said Bill. "And Toby, good luck. You're a brave lad."

Toby fumbled with the strange stick-like keys in the lock, eventually fiddling it open. Trying to be as quiet as possible, he swung the creaking door closed behind him and locked it. He crept out and up the steps, keeping an eye out for any raiders.

Maybe it'll be like Tash said at Fort George – maybe they'll be drunk by now.

He followed Bill's instructions, sliding down the slippery cobbled lane through a low tunnel that came out onto a large terrace. He tiptoed past the cottages on his left, in case there were any sleeping raiders inside. Then he set off fast across the knee-high grass, keeping low. Though the moon was on the wane, there was still enough light in the cloudless sky to illuminate the huge wall that wrapped around the castle. Toby headed towards it, searching for the gate.

Oh no! There are two sentries there. Capturing Bill must have put the raiders on alert.

He could see the stooping outlines of two men leaning against the wall, hiding from the cruel north wind in the lee of a buttress.

If I swing wide of them and approach from the south side, they won't see me or will they?

Toby silently encircled the gateway, keeping out of the men's line of sight. They were busy drinking from a bottle of something. When he reached the gate, his hands were shaking so much that he could hardly hold the skeleton keys.

Come on! Quick, before they see me!

The enormous padlock clicked open. Then he frantically tried to remove the chain without making a noise, but it was new and shiny and clinked and clanked against the iron gate.

"What's that?" shouted a surly voice. Toby froze.

"Ah, go away with yer. It's nothing but the ghosties rattling their chains in the graveyard!" yelled another. "Ha! You're a bit twitchy tonight, aren't you?"

Toby didn't hear the reply as the sentries turned their backs to him and snuggled further into the buttress to get out of the wind. He let out a deep breath: that was close. Luckily they seemed to be more interested in getting drunk then guarding the gate.

Having opened the gate for the soldiers to get in, he had to send the signal to let them know it was open. The best place would be up on the wall near the gate. Tom's soldiers must be waiting somewhere on the other side. He slunk into the far corner of the nether bailey and assessed the wall. It soared above him: twenty feet of greasy mossy stone. He would have to climb it freestyle, without ropes or protection. Toby tried to remember what his dad had taught him when they used to go climbing on the sea cliffs together.

Find a handhold first, then somewhere to put my foot, then another handhold...

Toby worked his way slowly up the imposing fortifications, stroking the stones to find crannies in which to push his hands and then pull himself up. He wriggled his foot to the right trying to find a foot-hold, slipping over the icy wet masonry.

I'm glad it's dark – can't see how far it is to the ground.

"Ouch!" He raked his frozen bare hand across the jagged stone, drawing blood.

Slowly but surely he scaled the ramparts, eventually heaving himself over the slimy edge at the top of the wall. It was surprisingly wide and had a line of battlements facing outwards. Toby stood up and turned on his torch. Using his body to shield the light from the castle side, he flicked it on and off in the SOS signal: dash, dash, dash, dot, dot, dot. He scanned the dark searching for an answering light.

They must be out there somewhere. Surely they'll send a signal back?

Over and over he signalled, bracing himself against the bitter wind and icy spindrift that blasted his face.

Come on! Where are you? I can't stay up here forever.

Just as he thought his finger was going to drop off, Toby spotted a flash of light twinkle in the depths of the valley below.

Hope they're not sending me a message – I won't be able to understand it. I only know the SOS in Morse code.

Toby waited until the flash had repeated several times and then, with a horrible lurch of his stomach, realised that he had to get down off the wall.

Wait a minute, if there are battlements up here then there must be some way for soldiers to get up onto them. All I need to do is walk along until I find it.

Toby half ran and half stumbled his way along the battlements, desperately searching for a way off. He'd almost gone past them when he spotted some steep steps leading into a courtyard. He groped his way carefully down, his feet slipping and sliding on the glassy ice-topped stones, until he reached the bottom.

Where am I now?

He could make out the silhouettes of tall buildings in front of him. He seemed to be in a small quadrangle behind the main courtyards. A narrow gravel path led towards an archway. Toby looked cautiously around; all was quiet, apart for the low moan of wind sweeping snow in from the north.

First, I've got to get Sylvie, Jamie and Katie. I hope they're not being guarded.

He swiftly made his way down the path and stood under the archway. He couldn't see any guards but they might be sheltering from the cold just inside. He would have to risk it. Keeping to the edge of the courtyard he made his way round to the Palace Hall where the women and children prisoners were being kept. He quickly unlocked the door; he was getting good at choosing the right skeleton key from the large bunch. Sneaking into the pitch-black hall, he called out softly,

"Sylvie? Jamie? Katie? It's Toby."

"I knew you'd come back for us," said a voice. Toby jumped. Sylvie was standing right beside him.

Gosh, she's got a lot of confidence in me. Better not let her down.

"I've got to find where they are keeping Dad," hissed Toby into the dark. A hand squeezed his arm; it was Jamie's mum stood on the other side of him. Jamie appeared next to her.

"Thanks for coming back for us," whispered Katie. "I think they're keeping your dad in the Great Hall where the General was. There are some rooms at the back, up some stairs."

Oh no. How are we supposed to get past him?

Toby heard someone stirring in their sleep, and then a cough and a snuffling noise.

"We need to get out of here before someone wakes up. We can't take them all with us just now. We'll have to come back for them later," said Toby, grabbing hold of Sylvie's hand. "And we have to be very quiet, eh, Sylvie? Come on!"

The four of them crept out of the door, first checking the courtyard for signs of any men. They silently crossed over to the great golden-coloured hall on the other side, and took refuge in the grand porch.

"We're so pleased you made it... it's been awful..." cried Jamie.

"Yes, Jamie, I know. I'm sorry, but we need to keep moving. A crack team of ex-SAS soldiers is about to descend on us any minute, and I need to rescue Dad before that happens," Toby explained as quickly as he could. "The soldiers are only after the General and his henchmen. I've left the door to the Palace Hall unlocked, so the people left behind have a chance to escape if they need to. We should try to let out the men prisoners, too, if we can."

I hope this plan works. What if the SAS guys start a battle and there's lots of shooting? We might not get out of here alive.

26. Dangerous Disobedience

Toby crept into the Great Hall, with Sylvie and the other two slinking in behind him. The spluttering candles threw a crazy glimmering light up the walls and ceiling, making strange-shaped shadows leap into the gloom. The hall was empty apart from the large lump of the General lying on a gigantic wooden table at the top end. The lump rose and shuddered with each exhale of a loud snore.

"Do you think he's drunk?" whispered Toby.

"More like he's sleeping off the effect of those drugs I doped him with," smiled Katie. "I gave him enough to knock out a horse. He won't be bothering us for a while."

"Really?" hissed Toby. "Wow! I knew you'd think of something. Was it the pachu berries?"

"There's no such thing. They were just some dried raspberries I put in to hide the taste of the sedatives. Glad I kept those drugs now, I knew they'd come in handy someday. I used to put them in bait for the dogs so that I could study them closely."

Cool! Jamie's mum is so cool.

"So how do we get to these rooms then?" asked Toby.

Katie led them to the right of a huge stone fireplace, where a velvet curtain hid a small door. It was bolted and locked. After a quick fiddle with the bunch of keys, Toby swung the door open.

"Dad? Are you in there?" Toby called out into the dark.

"He might be upstairs," suggested Katie. "The upstairs rooms butt onto the archway connecting this building to the Palace Hall where we were being kept."

"Is that the archway where I saw you at the window?" Toby asked Jamie.

"Yes. There's a door there but it was sealed up. We've been trying to open it to get to your dad," answered Jamie.

"Well, we don't need to now, providing his lordship here doesn't wake up," said Toby.

The four of them groped their way up a tiny narrow staircase that curved around, coming out into a tiny room at the top. There, curled up on the floor, wrapped in a nest of blankets, was Toby's dad. Toby couldn't believe that after all this time and all his trials and tribulations he had actually found him.

"Dad! Dad, it's me. It's Toby."

"Huh? What? Who's that? Toby? Is that you? Am I dreaming?" His dad poked his sleepy head out of the covers and blinked into the torchlight. "Good grief! It IS you! How did you find me? Sylvie? You managed to find Sylvie, too?"

"I told you Tobes would come and rescue us, didn't I, Daddy?" said Sylvie.

His dad staggered to his feet, and they all hugged, silly grins on their faces. Toby could see that his dad was trying hard not to cry but tears escaped down his grimy cheeks. Suddenly the sound that Toby dreaded most rang out through the night air:

HOOOOOOOOOOOOOOOOOOOOOOOOWL!

"The dogs? What are they doing here?" Toby gasped.

"We heard them earlier, didn't we, Mum?" cried Jamie.

"Yes, we've heard several howls tonight. They seem to be getting closer," said Katie.

"We'd better get a move on then. Dad, can you carry Sylvie? Let's go!" ordered Toby. "I'll explain as we go along, Dad. You see, the SAS are coming."

"What?" exclaimed his dad.

"Hush, and we'd better turn the torch off quick," warned Katie. "There could be guards going about."

Trying hard not to make any noise, the five of them carefully picked their way down the staircase in the dark, coming out into the Great Hall. The General still lay comatose on the table, snoring away.

Just then the main door swung open. In the dim light Toby saw several dark figures slink in, scanning the hall with their night goggles on, rifles raised to their shoulders. They ran in controlled smooth movements, crouching with their upper bodies still and alert, then disappearing into the shadows of the hall. It could only be the SAS team.

Just in time. I can get everyone out before any trouble kicks off.

He stepped forward into the flickering light of the candles.

"Tom, it's me. It's Toby," he called out, quietly. One of the figures held up his hand and the others halted.

"Toby? How did you get here? I thought you were still back at the bunker," said the black-clad figure. "And where is Bill? Wasn't it him sending the signal?"

"No, it was me," replied Toby. "Bill was captured, and his ankle got broken in the fight with the raiders. So I..."

"I underestimated you, Toby. I'm sorry. You're a very brave boy."

"Not really," said Toby, ruefully. "Just happen to be in the wrong place at the wrong time."

"So where's Bill now?" asked Tom.

"He's in the dungeon, next to the guardhouse," Toby told him.

Not moving from his stance, Tom signalled for two of his men to go and find Bill.

"And who are all these people?" Tom asked.

"I'm Toby's father, Dave Tennant, and this is his little sister, Sylvie, and this is Jamie," said Toby's dad, stepping closer to Toby.

"And I'm Katie McTavish, Jamie's mum." Katie walked towards Tom and offered her hand for him to shake.

"Nice to meet you. Look, this is all very well, but we're in the middle of a covert operation. We're here to secure the capture of the General." Tom's voice betrayed impatience.

"Well, there he is." Toby pointed to the slumped figure sprawled on the table. Tom signalled his men to move and take up positions. The six men lurking in the depths of the hall sped silently to surround the table, their gun muzzles pointing at the General.

"Katie's made your job easy: he's drugged. He won't give you any problems apart from having to move the big fatty," said Toby. "Now, if you'll excuse us we've got people to rescue."

"Oh, no you don't," commanded Tom, raising his rifle to point it at Toby and the others. "I can't take the risk of you and your family jeopardising this mission by alerting the raiders to our presence."

"Excuse me," cried Katie. "You can't keep us here against our will. That's... that's not right!"

"We should listen, Katie," interrupted Toby's dad. "We don't want to do anything to put these men at risk. What if we stay here until you've completed your mission and then we can go? After all, we want these raiders captured, don't we?"

Trust my dad to be on their side – he doesn't know these guys don't want to save anybody else because there's no room back at the bunker for them.

"You have my word, Mr Tennant. You'll be released as soon as we have all the General's men rounded up, and him and them safely removed."

"Ok. We'll stay here until you give us a signal it's safe to go," replied Toby's dad.

The men moved out stealthily, leaving one to guard the slumbering General, Toby and the others.

Toby slouched down against the wall in despair. This wasn't what he had imagined would happen. He wanted to leave the castle with all his family and friends, right now while there was a chance.

What if Tom's plan went wrong? They'd be stuck here with a very angry General and his disgruntled henchmen.

I can't let them stop me. I've come all this way to rescue Dad and Sylvie and just as I was about to get them out, we're risking being back in someone else's hands. I'm not going to sit here – I'm going to rescue everybody.

Toby thought of Tash and her parents. She was a good friend and a brave companion. He had intended to find her parents and take them back to the bunker to be reunited with her.

"I'm not staying here," he muttered to Jamie, who was slumped next to him. "Come on, let's sneak out and find the rest of the prisoners."

"Are you mad?" croaked Jamie. "We'll get pulverised by the SAS, and your dad will go mental!"

"Get a grip, Jamie," whispered his mum, who had slunk down beside the boys. "Your dad's busy with Sylvie. I'll cover for you, Toby. You go and let the rest of the prisoners out. Get yourselves back here in an hour. Go on. GO!"

Toby didn't wait; he ducked down and disappeared behind a bench. Jamie followed reluctantly.

"Honestly, my mum. What's she like?" grumbled Jamie. "Sometimes I wish she would act a bit more responsibly. What's all this commando stuff about?"

"Shh. Let's get going," hissed Toby, crawling behind a tapestry covering on the wall.

The two boys slipped out into the courtyard where there was no sign of Tom and his team, not even any footprints left in the snow.

"We've got to find where the men are being kept. Any ideas?" murmured Toby under his breath.

"I think the men are being held on the farm where we work every day. It's been horrible, Toby. The raiders have forced us to dig the fields and plant potatoes and stuff."

Toby could imagine how much Jamie would have hated that. Jamie disliked any physical activity. He'd much rather sit and read a book.

"They were seriously scary. They had guns and they used to crack whips at us and everything, and they didn't feed us – just yucky potato soup every day!"

I'm so glad I didn't get kidnapped!

"I think there's a whole lot of new sheds down in the valley bottom. I bet they're down there," said Jamie.

"Should we get the women and children out first or will the little ones be frightened and noisy?" wondered Toby.

His questions were interrupted by a loud explosion ripping through the archway leading to the other courtyard and blowing snow and dust into his face.

"What was that?" yelled Jamie.

"Tom's men must have thrown one of those smoke grenade things into the guardhouse to get the raiders out. We need a quick plan now. Things are going to get pretty wild around here!"

"I think I can hear the dogs again," exclaimed Jamie. "And it sounds like there's more. Could it be Cerberus and his pack?"

That flipping dog seems to follow me wherever I go!

"I don't know but we can't send the mums and kids down to the farm if the dogs are about – they won't stand a chance. Hang on, Jamie, what's that?"

Toby quickly grabbed Jamie and pulled him further into the shadows. The din of men running and shouting reverberated through the archway, echoing off the ancient walls. A black-clad figure rushed past them, a gun braced to his shoulder.

Sounds like Tom's men have underestimated the raiders. They're not going quietly.

"Jamie, I think we'll have to go and rescue the men prisoners ourselves. Things aren't going smoothly. We can't risk being here if Tom's mission goes wrong."

"What shall we do?"

"Let's get the men up to the castle and they can help the mums move the children safely, and quicker than we could on our own. We just have to get out into the car park first – then…" Toby wasn't sure what he'd do then. But he knew he had to somehow get the prisoners away from the raiders and the dogs. "Come on, Jamie. We need to move!"

"Really?" wailed Jamie. "Do we have to?"

"We've done dafter things than this. Remember, we once rescued your mum from under the nose of Cerberus!"

Jamie nodded in resignation.

I need him to be big and brave now. I wish Tash was here – she'd be up for it.

Jamie had obviously seen the determined look on Toby's face. "Ok, let's go." He stumbled out across the courtyard.

Toby reckoned they needed to get out the other side of the guardhouse and through the entrance gates. But how? They would have to get past the battle that seemed to be raging around the guardhouse. Was there another way round to the car park? At that moment he heard more shouting. He peered out and saw several darkly dressed figures struggling up the cobbled ramp, hauling some of the raiders behind them. The raiders had their hands fastened behind their backs, and were swearing and cursing.

"They've got some of them! Right, we're on the move!"

Toby kept in the shadow of the Palace Hall walls, skulking down the icy yard until he reached the gatehouse. It was empty. He didn't wait to check if Jamie was keeping up, just raced out across the first bridge. Sprinting through an archway, he crossed another bridge and into the large open space where the vehicles were parked.

"Toby!" yelled Jamie. "Wait for me!" But Toby kept on running. If the SAS had captured some of the raiders then maybe the other raiders would come to their defence and that would mean a fight. He didn't want to get caught in the middle.

There in the yard sat the white van he had arrived in. He dived into it. Jamie jumped into the passenger seat as Toby caught his breath.

"So, how are you going to start it? Do you know how to hot-wire it?" asked Jamie breathlessly.

"No, you dope, I'm going to use the keys." Toby flipped down the sun visor and out fell the keys to the van.

"That was clever. How did you know they were going to be there?"

"Call it intuition," replied Toby, turning the key in the ignition. He grinned at Jamie as he turned the van around and headed for the sentry post. The two raiders who had been there before had disappeared. The only obstacle was the wooden barrier across the entrance.

"Hold on!" shouted Toby as he put his foot to the floor. The van rammed the pole sending it bouncing over the ground. He swerved round a corner, slewing sideways over the icy tarmac, and headed down the hill.

"I think it's that way," yelled Jamie, pointing to a cobbled road on their left. Toby wrenched the steering hard and the van bucketed over the bumpy lane. Toby clenched his teeth and concentrated on keeping the van on the road as it slithered and skidded down into the valley below.

I only hope we get there before the dogs.

27. A Change of Heart

As the van's headlights picked up the huddle of farm steadings at the end of the bumpy track, Toby caught sight of swiftly moving shadows circling the perimeter fencing.

The dogs are here! Or is it the wolves?

"One of us will have to get out and open the gate," he said, glancing at Jamie's white face and clenched knuckles.

"I'll do it," whispered Jamie hoarsely.

"Ok – but you need to be quick! Leave the door open and I'll keep moving." Toby hoped that Jamie wouldn't lose his nerve.

He slowed the van down while Jamie flung open the door and jumped out, racing for the tall wire-mesh gates. Toby revved the van engine, hoping the noise would frighten off the dogs.

Hurry! Hurry Jamie!

How many dogs were there, lurking in the darkness? Toby tried not to stare past the beam of the lights. Instead, he kept his attention on Jamie struggling with the heavy bolts on the gates in front of the van.

Jamie finally managed to push the gates slowly open. Toby didn't wait, using the van to ram them.

"Close them, Jamie! Quick!" he bellowed, leaning across to shout out of the passenger door. He could see Jamie in the wing mirror, battling with both gates to bring them together. On the other side of the wire mesh, Toby could see something approaching, slinking low to the ground: shapes started to converge on Jamie.

"Jamie! The dogs! Come on! Leave the gates!" he shrieked. He could now see the glint of the dogs' eyes and the gleam of their fangs, which looked blood-red, bathed in the brake lights of the van.

"JAMIE!"

Jamie leapt at the gates and with one final effort slammed closed the bolts on the inside, just as a large dog jumped up.

"GET LOST!" Jamie shouted, as its muzzle bounced off the wire. He sprinted for the open van door, throwing himself through it. Before he was even half in, Toby sped off, one hand clutching Jamie's jacket.

"Did you see that? It nearly had me!" gasped Jamie, incredulously. "It was HUGE! Do you think they are Cerberus's followers?"

"Probably!" cried Toby. "They don't look friendly, that's for sure."

They sped down the track. The large sheds stood smartly in rows in a massive new yard complete with silos and open-sided stores full of farm machinery. There were combines, tractors, diggers, fork-lift trucks, harrows, seed drills, and slurry carts. All of them were parked silently in lines, waiting for fuel.

Wow – this place is enormous. It's a huge industrial-farm complex. So this is what the General has been building! And look at the equipment he's got – he must have been collecting it from all over Scotland.

"Look at all this gear!" he cried out to Jamie. "Why wasn't he using that instead of making you do the hard work?"

"He's a mad man, Toby!" yelled back Jamie. "He enjoyed watching us slaving in the fields. And anyway, my mum thought he was getting paranoid about running out of fuel. That's why he was so keen to find an engineer. He had this crazy idea of converting all these vehicles to electricity once he'd found a way to generate some."

Maybe not so crazy – there did used to be electric cars. Why not electric tractors?

"There!" Toby cried, spotting a large concrete barn with double doors. In front of the doors the snow and ice were rutted and marked with fresh footprints and machinery tracks. He veered to a halt and braked hard. He and Jamie sprang out of the van and sprinted to the doors.

"Anyone in there?" Toby banged on the doors with his fists. A muffled shout could be heard from within. "Help me, Jamie!" Toby yanked at the chain and padlock that held the doors fast. The skeleton keys would be no good here: the padlock was too small and modern.

Where's that hacksaw?

His hands shaking, Toby rummaged in his pockets and pulled out the hacksaw. He started sawing at the padlock. More shouts could be heard, and someone thumped on the metal barn door.

"We're coming!" yelled Jamie. "We're here to rescue you. Hold on, we've just got to saw off the lock! Get a move on, Toby, those dogs looked like they meant business. I don't think that gate will hold them for long."

What does he think I'm doing? Making jam? Honestly, Jamie!

It seemed to Toby to take an age, with him sawing as hard as he could at the padlock. But eventually the chain fell loose to the ground.

"It's off!" he cried, tugging at the handles. Someone on the other side was pulling and pushing, and the doors slid creakily open. There stood a dishevelled group of men, blinking into the headlights of the van. They were wearing filthy blue boiler suits, some had bushy beards and matted hair, some had old grey bandages wrapped around their hands. All of them were scarily thin.

Jamie grabbed Toby's arm. "They look terrible!" he whispered. Toby nodded.

Better get them to safety – they don't look like they could knock the skin off a rice pudding, never mind fight off the dogs.

"Open the back doors, and let's hope they'll all get in," he said quietly.

One of them strode forward. He looked healthier than the others.

"Hello, I'm Dan. We're glad to see you! But how on earth did two young lads get through all the raiders' defences? And where did —"

"I'll explain later," interrupted Toby. "We really need to get going. Things are kicking off big style. Can we get all these people in the van?"

Toby could see that Dan was looking strangely at him, not knowing whether to trust this wild-eyed boy who was dishing out orders. Then he nodded and began to help usher the rest of the men into the van while Jamie hovered nervously, jumping from one foot to the next.

"Come on! Don't want to stay here any longer... We've got to move fast!"

Toby slammed the van doors shut. Dan appeared next to him.

"I'll drive if you like," said Dan. "I used to be a rally driver before —"

"That's great!" exclaimed Toby. "The roads are dead slippy, and then there are the dogs to get past."

"Dogs? What dogs?" asked Dan, leaping into the driver's seat. As he backed the van away from the barn, Toby explained to him about the dogs.

"Well, they'd better not get in my way, 'cause I'm not stopping!" cried Dan. "Watch this!" He put his foot down hard and the van spun round and headed for the tall wire-mesh gates.

SMASH!

The gates buckled and bent under the impact from the van blasting through them. They burst open, knocking sideways a couple of dogs that had been barking ferociously at the approaching vehicle. Toby and Jamie clung onto the front seat as the vehicle careered up the rutted farm track and back onto the lane. Toby, yelling over the roar of the engine, told Dan about the SAS team having captured the raiders and their leader.

"Nasty piece of work, that General," Dan remarked, crashing the gears as he went round a bend. "I've not been here as long as the other guys, but from what I've seen he's not to be messed with. Seems he's very intelligent, though. He came up with this New Caledonia idea all by himself. And he's managed to organise this private army of his. Apparently they're planning to take over the whole of Scotland."

"Well, hopefully he won't be organising anyone after tonight," sighed Toby.

As they swung into the castle car park, Toby could see a haze of smoke hanging over the outer courtyard.

Are they still fighting? Or have all the raiders surrendered? Where are Tom and his men now?

"We'd better go straight to the Palace Hall. That's where they're keeping all the women and children," said Toby, as the van screeched to a halt in front of the main archway. "Keep an eye open for raiders, and dogs."

The men crawled out of the back of the van and made their way cautiously through the gateways and into the inner courtyard. Toby and Jamie kept an anxious watch. There was no sign of any people or any dogs. Dan and some of the men closed the heavy inner door, and bolted it shut.

"In here," instructed Toby, pushing open the door to the Palace Hall. "Bring everyone over to the Great Hall opposite as soon as you can get them all together."

Toby and Jamie left Dan and hurried across the courtyard. Toby checked his watch: they had been gone for over an hour. What had happened in their absence?

Inside the Great Hall it was dark. The flames from the candles had died leaving the cavernous interior lit only by small pools of light from the shielded torches of the SAS team. They were stood guarding a group of raiders who were sat on the floor with their hands bound. The General, still snoring, lay propped up against a pillar. Toby and Jamie entered hesitantly, unsure of how they'd be received.

"Ah! The wandering hero returns!" remarked Tom sarcastically. "And where have you been, Toby?"

"Me and Jamie have been rescuing the men, women and children, like YOU should have been!" Toby was defiant.

"Toby!" exclaimed his dad. "Don't be so cheeky to Tom. He's had his work cut out capturing this bunch. He doesn't need any grief from you. You could have jeopardised the entire mission!"

You could at least stand up for me, Dad. And you've not seen the state the prisoners are in...

"Our main priority is to capture these men," continued Tom. "We'll load them into the vehicles and get on our way."

"I don't think you should do that!" rang out a loud voice. Toby jumped in surprise as Jamie's mum stepped forward. "You can't leave all the people here defenceless," she continued. "What if the dogs get into the castle? What if some of the raiders come back after you've gone, and take over again?"

Yeah – go for it, Katie!

Toby edged over to stand next to her. She reminded him of his mum when she had got fired up over something she cared about. Her cheeks were bright red and her eyes were all ablaze..

"I'm sorry, Mrs McTavish, but my orders were to capture these men and remove them."

"But you said yourself you're not a military unit anymore, so you don't have to obey orders," remarked Toby. "And anyway, whose orders were they?"

Tom shifted uncomfortably on his feet and looked at Simon.

"Actually, they were my own orders," he said.

"So you can change them, can't you?" demanded Toby.

"Yes," said Katie, "there's nothing to stop you making new orders, is there?"

"Wait —" started Tom, but before he could say more, the door opened and Dan walked in followed by all the men and women and children. Toby could see from Tom's face that he was shocked by the state of them. As they limped in they looked as if all their spirit had been knocked out of them. The little ones were whimpering and crying, clutching onto their mums or trying to find their dads in the mêlée of adults that trooped into the hall.

Simon approached Tom and whispered urgently in his ear. Toby could see that some argument was taking place and finally Tom, with a resigned look, nodded.

"Ok, we're agreed, we can't leave these people here like this, but we can't offer them permanent shelter either. If we take them back to the bunker and get them well and strong again, then they must agree to leave after that. How about that?"

"That'll be fine!" called out Dan. "On behalf of everyone here, I think we will be happy to accept your offer. We'll leave to start up a New Caledonia of our own as soon as we are able to. Who knows, we may come back here? The General has put some serious thought into organising this place – there are crops growing in the fields, and cows and sheep at pasture. There's even fresh water and a sewerage system."

"Ok, so that's settled, then. I'll send some of my men for vehicles. They're just outside the castle walls on the west side," said Tom, trying to look like he was still in control.

"Toby!" a small voice rang out and Sylvie dashed from behind her dad and grabbed Toby around his knees. "Toby, you're so big and brave! You came back to save Dad and me! And look!" Sylvie opened the top of her jacket to show a small furry face peeking from within it.

"Ha! Henry!" laughed Toby. "You managed to save Henry. You're brave, too, Sylvie." Toby knelt down and hugged his little sister, being careful not to squash Henry. His dad was looking down at him.

"I'm so proud of you, Toby. I didn't realise there were all these people in such a bad way. You saved them all. You're a real hero, Toby," said his dad, putting an arm around his son. "You're my hero."

"Thanks, Dad. It wasn't just me, though – there was Tash and then Jamie... and if it hadn't been for Tash's great-grandma, who was a heroine in World War Two, I would never have been able to unlock the —" Toby stopped, he was starting to choke up with relief.

"It's ok, Toby, it's going to be all right now," interrupted his dad. "We thought you had drowned when you jumped off the boat. I don't know how you survived that. We never thought we'd see you again."

Just then Toby heard something that made his blood freeze: a solitary howl resounded through the cold walls of the castle.

Cerberus? He sounds very close – are the dogs in the castle?

Then another howl rang out, but this one was different. It was a deeper, rougher howl, coming from the other direction.

The wolves?

"I think we should all leave immediately. There's going to be trouble," declared Toby, picking up Sylvie.

We must get out of here, now.

28. The Battle of Stirling Castle

"We must go!" Toby cried. He lurched down the hall, holding tight to Sylvie, pushing his way through the throng of people. Panic was tightening its grip on him. He could feel the fear rising in his throat.

"Toby?" cried his dad, racing after him. "What is it? Toby, you're scaring Sylvie. Slow down!"

She'll be a lot more scared if she sees those dogs. Got to get her out of here fast.

He staggered to the main door, feeling his legs turning to jelly as he fought for breath.

"Toby!" shouted Tom. "Stop!" The command rang across the hall. Toby collapsed into a heap, letting Sylvie slip slowly from his arms. Tom strode towards him and helped him to his feet.

"We're not going to let the dogs do any harm, don't worry," said Tom reassuringly. "I take your concerns seriously. I know that these are no ordinary dogs. We'll get you all into the vehicles and go." He put his arm around Toby and led him to a bench. Toby sat with his head in his hands, shaking violently.

As he felt the panic slowly subsiding, Toby lifted his head and looked around. There were adults standing talking quietly in anxious groups.

Tash's parents should be here somewhere. At least, I really hope they are.

Toby suddenly remembered something. Stuffed in the bottom of his jeans pocket were the photographs he and Tash had taken at Christmas at the Kingshouse Hotel. He fished out a screwed-up print and tried to smooth the creases. From the crumpled paper smiled Tash, her jet-black hair framing her face and a wide smile showing her pearly white teeth.

Toby got to his feet and wandered over to some of the adults.

"Do you know this girl?" he asked. "Her name is Natasha, but her friends call her Tash." The weary folk shook their heads.

Toby approached a couple sitting on the floor near the door. The grave-looking man was talking quietly in a foreign language to a small frail woman with a brightly coloured silk scarf covering her head. As he got near, Toby could see she had black hair streaked with white poking out from under the scarf.

"You must be Tash's parents?" he cried, shoving the photo in front of them. The woman took it in trembling hands and burst into tears, babbling something incoherently to her husband.

"You know our Natasha?" said the man, incredulously. "Where did you get this photo?"

"Yes!" cried Toby. "I know Tash, she's my friend. We travelled from Fort George together. She's safe, don't worry. She's at the bunker where Tom is taking us. You'll see her soon."

Tash's dad wrapped his arms around Toby, smothering him in a huge hug. Her mum stood up and joined in, squeezing Toby in an enveloping embrace.

"We never thought we see our Natasha again..." sobbed her dad. "Her mother says you must be brave boy to save her. We see her soon, yes?"

Toby nodded and gulped hard. He could feel all the emotion of the day starting to well up inside of him.

"Yes," he cried. "You see her soon!" The three of them burst out laughing, as they stood holding onto each other.

Toby's dad came over with Sylvie and Toby introduced them to Tash's parents. The five of them sat in a small huddle, shaking hands and trying to chat calmly about how they came to be there.

Just then the main doors swung open and a balaclava-clad soldier stood waving his rifle in the air, signalling them all to move.

"Come on, everybody!" shouted Tom. "Let's get loaded up as quickly as possible."

The sun was dappling the courtyard in a sharp bright light as Toby stepped, blinking, outside. A new day had started while they had been hiding in the Great Hall, and a cold dry wind chased across the turreted walls. In the courtyard the raiders and the General were being thrown unceremoniously into the back of the white van, their faces dark with anger and frustration. Next to the van was parked a fleet of army trucks, their engines running and their doors open.

"Tom?" asked Toby, "can I ride shotgun up front in the cab?"

"Yes, sure. You really want to? Might be a bit scary."

"Huh! I'm not scared, really," replied Toby. Tom smiled and shrugged.

"Ok. Go with Simon in that one."

Toby watched as his dad and Sylvie got into the back of one of the trucks, along with Tash's parents, Jamie, and Jamie's mum. He then climbed into the front with Simon.

"Let's get this show on the road!" cried Simon, driving out of the yard, under the archway and into the inner courtyard. Travelling fast over the outer bridges, they were soon in the huge car park. Simon pulled over to the left to miss the smashed security barrier. As he did so, Toby could see over the embattlements, down to the valley beneath them.

"STOP!" Toby shouted. "LOOK!" He signalled frantically for Simon to pull in.

Simon swerved to bring the truck to the edge of the esplanade so they could see the whole plain spread out below them for miles and miles. From the castle perched high on the rocky ridge, the land spilled higgledy-piggledy down, spanning out at the bottom into rich flat farmland. Toby saw the work that had been done by the prisoners: square fields of neat, black, ploughed earth, plots of vegetables, lines of sown cereals and paddocks full of cows and sheep grazing. Surrounding all the acres of land was a huge fence made of wood and barbed wire with a wooden watchtower at every corner.

But it wasn't any of this that had caught Toby's attention. As he had glanced across the vista he saw the pattern of light changing, dappling the fields below, as something moved at speed over the land. It was something dark and disturbing.

Like a black tide. It's a black tide of dogs!

Out in front of the wave upon wave of sleek black dogs, a solitary animal was racing along, his head held high, his stubby tail erect.

Cerberus!

"LOOK!" cried Simon, pointing to the far left of the castle. From the other side of the Carse of Stirling came another flow of movement. Toby strained to see what was moving: it was another tide of animals and it was heading straight for Cerberus and his pack. These beasts were bigger and rangier, with mottled-grey hairy coats. Out at their front, galloping towards Cerberus, sped a huge grey wolf.

There's going to be a battle – the dogs against the wolves! Cerberus must be mad if he thinks he can win – they look even scarier than him and his pack.

"I think we should go quickly. We don't want to get caught up in this," said Simon. "They might decide to unite against their common enemy: humans."

Toby nodded speechlessly, not able to take his eyes off the appalling scene unfolding in the valley. As the two dark shadows converged towards each other, the cows and sheep took fright and fled towards the hills in blind panic.

Simon reversed back onto the road and joined the line of trucks that was zooming out of the car park.

"WAIT!" Toby shrieked again. "Let me out! I've just seen something!"

Simon braked hard, slewing the truck across the snowy gravel, as Toby flung the truck door open.

"What are you doing?" cried Simon. "We've got to travel in convoy, we mustn't lose the others." But Toby didn't hear him; he was pelting across the tarmac. He had seen a shadowy white shape moving fast through the cemetery that ran alongside the car park.

"Belle! Belle! Come here!" he shouted. Jamie's big, white, fluffy dog was bounding towards him. "Belle – it's Toby – come – good girl!" She bounced up to him, jumping around and wagging her tail furiously, her large pink tongue licking at his face and hands. She was so happy to see him.

"And I'm happy to see you, too, Belle. Come on, let's go and find Katie and Jamie!"

The two of them sprinted back to the truck, Belle almost knocking Toby over in her excitement. Toby pulled open the back door.

"Look who I've found!" he yelled, as Belle leapt in.

"BELLE!" cried Jamie and his mum, simultaneously.

"Hurry up, Toby!" screamed Simon from the front. "We've got to get going!"

Toby climbed back into the truck, a huge grin on his face. He couldn't believe that Belle had managed to survive so long on her own, despite the wild dogs and the wolves. It must have been Belle trying to play with Bill in the graveyard when he'd tried to sneak into the castle. Only Belle would be daft enough to want to play ball with a stranger in the middle of the night.

"You're mad, you are," said Simon, though he was smiling, too.

"I know. Just what we need, eh? Another dog!"

The convoy of trucks tore along the lanes leading from the castle, bumped over the cobbled streets of Stirling, then swung right out of the town centre to avoid the Carse where the dogs and wolves were doing battle.

As the truck sped along country lanes heading away from Stirling, Toby settled down in his seat. He felt the adrenalin that had been coursing so fast through his veins start to ebb away, leaving him drained and his limbs heavy. He was beginning to feel very very tired.

"How long will it take to get to the bunker?" he asked Simon, yawning.

But before he heard the answer he was fast asleep.

29. Forward to the Future

Toby woke to Simon gently shaking him.

"We here already?" he asked sleepily, climbing stiffly out of the cab. His dad was walking down the ramp into the bunker, carrying a soundly sleeping Sylvie. Belle came rushing up, all tongue and tail, her body gyrating with happiness, followed by a grinning Jamie.

"Oh, Toby! I can't thank you enough. That was amazing! Fancy spotting Belle like that. I thought she had..."

"Well, she hadn't, and lucky for you I've got good eyesight. Now, where are Tash's mum and dad? I must take them to see her. She'll still be in the medical bay."

"So this Tash you've been talking about – is she your best friend now?" asked Jamie.

"Don't be daft, Jamie, you can both be my best friends! After all, it's not like I've got a lot of them."

"That's ok then, just wanted to know."

Toby patted his friends arm and hobbled off to find Tash's parents.

Tash was sitting up in bed when Toby finally arrived at the medical bay with her parents in tow.

"Hello, lazy bones," he said. "Look who I've brought to see you."

"Father! Mother!" cried Tash. Snowy got up from under the bed and greeted Tash's dad enthusiastically, baring his teeth in a grin and wagging his huge tail.

"You'd think he'd known you all his life," said Toby, amazed.

"He recognises someone who knows something about wolves," Tash told him. "And YOU are a very bad boy, going off and leaving me here," she cried, laughing through her tears of happiness.

Tash's parents crowded excitedly around the bed, hugging and kissing their long-lost daughter, and chattering in what Toby presumed must be Russian. He left discreetly; he could see it was a very emotional reunion. He told Tash he'd come back later and relate all of his adventure. As he left, he saw that Snowy was lying at Tash's dad's feet, staring up at him in adoration.

Toby found his dad sitting in the canteen with Jamie, Katie and Tom. They were all tucking into huge platefuls of breakfast. Belle was lying under the table, slurping down a large bowl of custard.

"This place is amazing," enthused Jamie, stuffing a large piece of bread into his mouth. "I haven't had any proper food for ages."

"Go steady! You'll make yourself sick," advised Toby, picking at some toast.

"Jamie," said Katie, kindly, "why don't you take Toby to see Sylvie. We adults need to discuss the future."

"Don't we have any say in the future?" demanded Jamie. "Toby here has rescued all of us practically single-handed. I think you should ask him what he wants to do."

"It really is ok, Jamie, I've told you before," sighed Toby, "I'm so tired of making decisions. It's too worrying. I'm quite happy for the adults to take over now. Let's go and see Sylvie and Henry."

The two boys found Sylvie sitting on the edge of her bed cuddling the little brown rabbit.

"Hello Sylve, how's Henry? Has he recovered from his adventure?" asked Toby, patting the rabbit's soft fluffy fur as he sat down on the bed. "Ouch! What's this?" he exclaimed. "There's something hard under here."

Toby put his hand under the duvet and removed a small cloth bag containing some heavy objects that made a clacking noise. He pulled open the drawstring fastening and put his hand in.

"Mum's marble eggs!" he cried, taking out a smooth, round, egg-shaped object. "Where did you get these from?"

"Daddy's had them all the time. He always carries them with him. He gave them to me to play with this morning, but I had to promise to be very careful with them."

"I'll say – these are the only things we have left that were Mum's. I thought we'd left them in the cottage at Collieston. I'm glad Dad remembered to bring them with him."

"Me too," said Sylvie, holding a shiny, pink marble egg in her hand. "They're very pretty, and they remind me of Mummy."

Toby tried to think of some way of changing the subject; he didn't want Sylvie to get upset. Then he remembered something. "Hold on, I've got something for you!" he shouted, running from the room. He returned minutes later clutching a box.

"Here, a present for you," he said, watching Sylvie's excited face.

"What is it, Tobes?"

He saw her expression turn to disbelief.

"You found it! It's *The Little Mermaid*!"

"I promised you, didn't I? Maybe they'll have a DVD player here. They've got just about everything else. I'll go and ask someone."

Later, Toby, Jamie, Tash and Sylvie sat on the bed watching the film in silence.

This is great – safe at last. And Sylvie has her favourite film. Who'd have thought I'd have found that in this mad world?

Toby put his arm around Sylvie who snuggled up to him. Tash turned and smiled at them both.

"Look what Bill gave me," she said, laughing. She held up a dirty, tatty-looking teddy bear.

"Who would think a seriously scary soldier like Bill would rescue a teddy bear in the midst of a battle?" remarked Jamie.

"Just shows you," said Toby. "You should never judge people by their outward appearances, after all who'd think a brave wolf-girl would even have a teddy bear!"

They all laughed, especially Tash.

I hope Tash gets on with Jamie – then I'd have two friends. I miss all my school friends. No, don't think about that. Think forwards to the future.

"Eh, Henry, stop nibbling my jumper!" cried Sylvie, pulling a long thread from the rabbit's paws. Henry sat up on the bed and started to wash his ears.

They all burst out laughing once more.

"I'm so glad I got to see *The Little Mermaid* again," mumbled Sylvie.

"Me too," said Toby.

"You said it was for babies!" declared Sylvie indignantly.

"Yeah, it is, but sometimes it's nice to go back to being a baby," Toby said. "This adult stuff is too much like hard work."